Perfect Victim

Michael Ferguson

Published by Michael Ferguson, 2024.

PERFECT VICTIM

First edition. September 9, 2024.

Copyright © 2024 Michael Ferguson.

ISBN: 979-8227479198

Written by Michael Ferguson.

Table of Contents

Chapter 1: The Perfect Case

The evening light filtered through the large bay windows of Catherine Faber's pristine office, casting golden hues on her bookshelf, each title a reflection of her professional success. On the shelf stood her most recent accomplishment, Breaking Free: A Woman's Guide to Escaping Abuse, now a national bestseller. Catherine gazed at the cover for a moment, taking in the image of a woman stepping through an open door, a symbol of liberation. In many ways, it reflected her own journey from her troubled past to the top of her field, but lately, something unsettled her. She dismissed it as a fleeting thought and reminded herself that she was helping people.

The world saw Catherine as a savior. A highly respected psychologist, she had dedicated her life to aiding women in abusive relationships, giving them the tools to break free. Her practice, based in a sleek building in Manhattan, was booming, thanks in part to her highly publicized work with Vanessa Hale. Vanessa's case had been a media sensation, a glamorous socialite trapped in a gilded cage of abuse, her controlling husband Evan Hale, a powerful real estate magnate, seemingly untouchable—until Catherine came into the picture.

Vanessa's testimony had been damning. She spoke of manipulation, fear, and isolation, painting a picture of emotional and psychological warfare that left the public in an uproar. With Catherine at her side, Vanessa became a symbol of empowerment, and Catherine, the hero who led her out of the darkness.

Sitting at her desk now, Catherine scrolled through her emails. The praise had been endless. Offers for interviews, television appearances, book deals—everyone wanted a piece of the woman who had freed Vanessa Hale. But beneath the surface, a small, nagging voice whispered doubts. Had Vanessa's story been too perfect? Was it possible Catherine had... helped shape it in ways that weren't entirely ethical?

No. Catherine pushed the thought away. Vanessa had been a victim—she was sure of it. And even if there had been some embellishment, the truth of the abuse remained. Didn't it?

Her assistant, Maria, knocked gently and peeked through the door. "Dr. Faber, you have a visitor. It's Vanessa Hale."

Catherine straightened, smoothing her blouse. "Send her in."

Vanessa swept into the room with the elegance and poise of someone born into wealth. She wore a designer dress, her blonde hair perfectly styled, yet there was a hardness to her that Catherine had noticed before. Today, though, it was more pronounced. Vanessa's face, usually composed and gracious, seemed tense.

"Vanessa, it's good to see you. How are you holding up?" Catherine gestured to the plush chair across from her desk, the one reserved for high-profile clients.

Vanessa sat but didn't answer right away. Instead, she looked out the window, her jaw clenched.

"I'm fine, Catherine. Or at least, I'm trying to be," Vanessa finally replied, her voice low but steady.

Catherine nodded sympathetically. "That's understandable. This process is difficult, but you're strong. You're taking the steps to reclaim your life."

Vanessa turned to face her, and for the first time since they'd started working together, Catherine felt an odd distance between them. Vanessa's gaze was sharp, almost... assessing.

"Am I?" Vanessa asked, her voice carrying an edge Catherine wasn't used to. "Because I'm starting to feel like I don't know what's real anymore."

A chill crept up Catherine's spine. She leaned forward, her brow furrowing. "What do you mean by that?"

Vanessa hesitated, running her fingers through her hair, her polished demeanor faltering. "I just—there are things I'm remembering now, things that don't quite fit. You know how trauma can distort memory, right? It's... confusing."

Catherine's pulse quickened. She had encountered clients doubting their own experiences before—it wasn't unusual. But something about the way Vanessa phrased her doubts felt different. More pointed. She chose her next words carefully.

"Trauma can absolutely affect memory," Catherine said gently. "But that's why it's important we talked through every detail. Your experiences are valid, Vanessa. Abuse isn't always obvious, and abusers are skilled at making you question your reality."

Vanessa's lips tightened into a thin line. "Right," she said, nodding, though her expression remained skeptical. "Right."

Catherine kept her face calm, but inside, a storm of anxiety was brewing. She couldn't afford for Vanessa to unravel now. The case had been too public, the spotlight too bright. If Vanessa started doubting herself, it could destroy everything they had worked for—everything Catherine had built.

The moment passed, and Vanessa finally sighed, standing up. "I'm just tired, Catherine. Maybe I'm overthinking things."

Catherine stood as well, moving toward Vanessa with a reassuring smile. "You're under a lot of pressure. It's normal to have doubts. But remember, you're strong. You've come so far, and no matter what, I'm here for you."

Vanessa nodded, but her expression remained distant. "Thanks. I should go—I have an event tonight."

Catherine watched as Vanessa turned and left, the sound of her heels clicking down the hall fading as quickly as it had come. When the office was silent again, Catherine sank into her chair, her heart pounding. Something had changed in Vanessa, and Catherine didn't like it.

She reached for her phone, dialing the number she knew by heart. After two rings, the familiar voice of her colleague, Dr. Laura Ellison, answered.

"Catherine, what's going on?" Laura asked, her voice warm with concern.

"I think I need to talk," Catherine said quietly, glancing out the window, her mind racing. "About Vanessa. And about... everything."

The line was silent for a moment before Laura spoke again. "Come by tonight. We'll have wine and figure it out."

Catherine agreed, but as she hung up, she couldn't shake the feeling that Vanessa's doubts were only the beginning. And if her most high-profile case started to crumble, how many others might follow?

That evening, Catherine found herself seated in Laura's cozy living room, a glass of red wine in hand. Laura, a fellow psychologist who had often acted as Catherine's sounding board, sat across from her, listening intently as Catherine recounted her conversation with Vanessa.

"So, she's doubting her own story now?" Laura asked, her brow furrowed. "That's concerning."

Catherine nodded, swirling the wine in her glass absentmindedly. "I don't know what to make of it. Vanessa's case was so clean, so textbook. But now... I don't know. She seemed distant. Almost suspicious of me."

Laura leaned forward, resting her elbows on her knees. "Catherine, do you think it's possible you... influenced her narrative more than you should have?"

The question hung in the air like a heavy cloud. Catherine felt a pang of defensiveness, but she also knew Laura wasn't accusing her—she was just asking the question Catherine had been avoiding.

"I don't think so," Catherine said slowly, but even to her, the words felt uncertain. "I mean, I guided her, of course. But isn't that what I'm supposed to do? Help her see the truth?"

Laura's expression softened. "Yes, but there's a fine line between helping someone recognize their reality and... creating one for them."

The room fell into a contemplative silence. Catherine took a sip of her wine, the bitter taste lingering on her tongue. Was it possible she had crossed that line? Could she have inadvertently led Vanessa down a path that wasn't entirely hers?

"I need to talk to her again," Catherine said finally. "I need to make sure she's okay. And that I didn't... push her."

Laura nodded. "That's a good idea. But be careful, Catherine. If Vanessa starts questioning things publicly, this could all blow up in your face."

Catherine knew Laura was right. She had to handle this delicately. One wrong move, and everything she had worked for could come crashing down.

As she left Laura's house that night, the city lights flickering around her, Catherine couldn't shake the growing sense of dread. For the first time in her career, she wasn't sure if she was the hero—or the villain.

The night was unnervingly quiet, the kind of silence that crept under your skin, pulling you back to moments you'd long tried to bury. Catherine Faber sat at her desk, bathed in the glow of her computer screen. She was supposed to be basking in triumph. Vanessa Hale's court victory was the final stroke in a masterpiece of justice she had curated with surgical precision. But instead of feeling elated, a strange sense of unease gnawed at her. As she glanced at the stack of congratulatory emails from colleagues and media inquiries asking for interviews, Catherine couldn't shake the subtle tug at the back of her mind. Something was off, something more than the inevitable backlash from those who believed she had overstepped her role.

Her fingers absentmindedly traced the edge of a framed photo on her desk—one that had remained turned face-down for years. Her mother, smiling faintly, was caught in the frame, the light in her eyes a stark contrast to the dark reality Catherine knew existed behind that smile. Catherine inhaled sharply and pushed the frame away, as if doing so could keep the memories at bay.

She closed her eyes, but the image of her father flooded in. His voice, cold and calculating, echoed in the recesses of her mind. "You're too sensitive, Catherine. That's why you'll always be weak." His words were seared into her like a brand. She had spent years fighting that weakness, building herself up, proving that she was strong—stronger than him, stronger than any of the men who dared to hurt women. But the memories still gnawed at her, threatening to unravel the control she fought so hard to maintain.

Catherine stood abruptly, as though physical movement could shake off the unease. She paced her office, her gaze drifting across the bookshelves lined with psychology texts and framed accolades. They were her armor, the things that told the world she was a woman in control. But deep down, she knew she wasn't. Not completely. Control was an illusion she projected to others, and often to herself.

She leaned against the window, looking out over the city. From here, the world appeared orderly, clean—people going about their lives, unaware of the messes hidden behind closed doors. She had made a career of opening those doors, exposing the truth. Yet the truth of her own life was a door she kept firmly shut.

The door to her office creaked open. David, her husband, stepped in. He had always had that quiet, steady presence about him, the kind that could fill a room without a word. "Still working?" His voice was soft, but laced with concern.

Catherine nodded, forcing a smile. "Just finishing up."

David's brow furrowed slightly. "You sure? You seem... distant."

Catherine turned away from the window. "It's just the case. Vanessa's victory. It's a lot to process."

David crossed the room, his footsteps slow, deliberate. He stopped just short of her, his eyes searching hers. "You don't have to carry it all on your own, you know?"

Catherine's throat tightened. He had said this before, and each time, the same response came up. "I'm fine." The lie tasted bitter, but she had gotten so good at it, she almost believed it herself.

David sighed, the familiar defeat in his expression. "Okay," he said softly, "but don't push yourself too hard." He pressed a kiss to her forehead, a gesture that felt both comforting and distant. "I'll be in bed."

Catherine watched him leave, the door closing softly behind him. Alone again, she returned to her desk, but instead of focusing on the stack of papers waiting for her attention, her mind drifted.

Her father's voice echoed louder now, pulling her back to the nights when she sat, a small child, watching her mother try to hold it together under the weight of his manipulation. "You're too weak," he had always said. "Too weak to save her." Catherine clenched her fists, the familiar burn of rage and helplessness flickering beneath the surface. She had sworn that she would never be weak again, never let another woman suffer what her mother had.

But that vow, that determination to save every woman who crossed her path, had blurred into something else over the years. A part of her knew she wasn't just helping them. She was reshaping their narratives, guiding them into seeing what she wanted them to see—what she needed them to see. Because if she could save them, then maybe, in some small way, she could rewrite the past. Maybe she could have saved her mother.

A sharp knock at the door snapped Catherine out of her thoughts. Startled, she looked up to see her assistant, Beth, standing hesitantly in the doorway.

"Sorry to bother you, but I thought you'd want to see this," Beth said, holding out her phone. "There's an article trending about the case. It's... well, it's not great."

Catherine took the phone, her stomach twisting. The headline read: "Vanessa Hale's Tale: A Heroic Escape or Fabricated Drama?"

Her chest tightened as she skimmed the article. It wasn't outright accusing Vanessa of lying, but it raised enough doubt to be dangerous. Subtle phrases like "inconsistencies in her testimony" and "questions surrounding the validity of her claims" stood out like flashing red lights. And worse, the article implied that Catherine may have played a role in shaping Vanessa's story, pushing her to exaggerate the abuse.

Catherine's hands trembled slightly as she handed the phone back to Beth. "It's nothing. Just speculation."

Beth hesitated, her brow furrowing in concern. "Should we respond? Maybe get ahead of it?"

"No," Catherine said, too quickly. She took a deep breath, forcing her voice to steady. "It'll blow over. They're just trying to stir up controversy."

Beth nodded, though she didn't look convinced. "Alright, just let me know if you change your mind."

As Beth left, the door clicked shut again, leaving Catherine in the silence once more. This time, the silence wasn't unsettling—it was suffocating. The article had struck a nerve, one she had been trying to ignore for weeks. There were inconsistencies in Vanessa's story, details that didn't quite add up. But Catherine had pushed them aside, convinced they were minor. After all, trauma affected memory. It was normal for a victim's recollection to be fragmented, confused. That's what she told herself, anyway.

But what if... Catherine's breath caught in her throat. What if those inconsistencies weren't just the result of trauma? What if Vanessa had lied? What if Catherine had been too eager to believe her, too desperate to see the parallels with her own life? What if, in trying to save Vanessa, she had pushed her too far?

Catherine shook her head, trying to dispel the thoughts, but they clung to her like shadows. You did the right thing. You always do. That was her mantra, the thing that kept her moving forward. But now, for the first time in a long time, she wasn't so sure.

She leaned back in her chair, closing her eyes, and let the memories wash over her—the nights spent hiding from her father's rage, the whispered apologies from her mother, the guilt that had haunted her for years. And beneath it all, a question that had been buried deep in her subconscious: Had she really saved her mother, or had she failed her?

As the night stretched on, the weight of that question settled heavy in her chest.

Chapter 2: Vanessa's Story

Vanessa Hale strode into Catherine Faber's office like a woman accustomed to being admired. Her tall frame was elegant, every movement deliberate, as if she were aware of the eyes that always followed her, even in private. Catherine observed her with the trained eye of someone who had seen hundreds of women in distress. But there was something about Vanessa, something compelling beneath the surface. As Vanessa sat down, her demeanor shifted slightly, the confidence cracking just enough to let the vulnerability peek through. She looked around Catherine's modest, yet inviting office, trying to mask the uncertainty beneath her carefully constructed mask of confidence.

Catherine waited, as she always did. Her clients usually filled the silence on their own. She knew Vanessa would be no different.

Vanessa sighed, running a manicured hand through her perfectly styled blonde hair. "I don't know where to start," she whispered, her voice betraying the years of turmoil she had kept hidden. "I've been married to Evan for almost a decade, and on the surface, it probably looks perfect." She laughed bitterly. "But it's far from it."

Catherine leaned forward, her soft gaze focused intently on Vanessa, a habit she'd perfected over years of counseling. She knew when to speak and when to let her clients unravel their tangled thoughts at their own pace. Today, she chose the latter.

Vanessa took a deep breath and continued. "I was a trophy wife. He never let me forget it. To the world, I was the beautiful wife of Evan Hale, the successful businessman, the socialite who appeared in magazines, photographed at charity galas. But behind closed doors..." Her voice wavered, the words struggling to come out. "Behind closed doors, it was different."

Catherine nodded slowly, signaling that she was listening, that Vanessa was safe to continue. She knew how to make her clients feel comfortable, how to coax the truth out of them, or at least what they believed to be the truth.

"Evan's always been controlling," Vanessa went on. "It started with little things. He'd tell me what to wear, where to go, how to act in public. It seemed like he was just looking out for me, at first. But then it got worse. He didn't want me to have friends. He monitored my calls, my messages. It was suffocating." Vanessa's voice cracked. "And when I tried to stand up to him, when I tried to push back, he'd..." She hesitated.

Catherine's gaze sharpened slightly, sensing what was coming. "Did he hurt you physically, Vanessa?"

Vanessa's eyes welled up with tears. "Not at first. It was more... psychological. He'd manipulate me, make me feel like I was nothing without him. He'd isolate me from everyone I cared about, make me doubt myself. I started believing it, Catherine. I started believing I was nothing."

Catherine felt a chill run down her spine, her own memories beginning to surface, but she pushed them back. This wasn't about her. "It's not your fault," she said softly. "You've been through trauma. Psychological abuse can be just as damaging, if not more, than physical abuse."

Vanessa wiped away her tears, nodding as though she needed to hear that, needed someone to tell her it wasn't her fault. But then, as she continued, the story took a darker turn.

"It got physical about two years ago. We were at some charity event, and I was talking to one of Evan's business partners. He didn't like that. When we got home, he accused me of flirting with him." Vanessa's voice dropped to a whisper. "He grabbed my wrist so hard I thought it would break. He threw me across the room like I was nothing."

Catherine's hands tightened slightly in her lap, though her expression remained calm. She'd seen this before—abusers who escalated from psychological manipulation to physical violence. She had dealt with it professionally, and in her past, she had been a victim herself, though she rarely acknowledged it.

"What did you do after that?" Catherine asked gently.

"I stayed," Vanessa admitted, her voice filled with shame. "I stayed because I didn't know what else to do. I was afraid. Evan's powerful, Catherine. He's connected. If I left, if I told anyone, who would believe me? And even if they did, what could they do against someone like him?"

It was a familiar story. Catherine had heard it countless times before, though Vanessa's case had the added complexity of wealth and social standing. The stakes were higher, the risk of public humiliation greater.

"I'm here now because I can't take it anymore," Vanessa continued. "I can't live like this. I want out. I need your help."

Catherine nodded, her professional mind already working through the details, figuring out how to navigate the situation. Vanessa's story was compelling, heartbreaking even. But Catherine had learned to be cautious. Even the most credible-seeming stories had their complications, their nuances. And while Vanessa appeared to be a victim of abuse, Catherine knew better than to take things at face value.

"I believe you, Vanessa," Catherine said, her voice steady. "And I want to help you. But before we move forward, I need to ask you some difficult questions. Are you sure there's nothing you're holding back? Any details, even minor ones, that you haven't shared yet?"

Vanessa looked down at her lap, her fingers fidgeting with the hem of her dress. "There are things I haven't told you yet," she admitted after a long pause. "But it's not because I'm hiding anything. It's just... it's hard to talk about."

Catherine leaned back in her chair, her eyes narrowing slightly as she considered Vanessa's words. There was something about the way Vanessa spoke, the way she chose her words carefully, that raised a flag in Catherine's mind. It wasn't unusual for victims to withhold information out of shame or fear, but there was something else going on here. Something deeper.

"Take your time," Catherine said softly. "I'm here to listen when you're ready."

Vanessa nodded, her expression a mixture of relief and apprehension. She had come to Catherine for help, but she clearly wasn't ready to lay everything on the table just yet.

Catherine could sense that there was more to Vanessa's story—more than what she was willing to reveal in that moment.

As the session drew to a close, Catherine gave Vanessa her personal contact information, a rarity for her. "Call me if you need anything," Catherine said, her tone gentle but firm. "We'll get through this together."

Vanessa nodded, taking the card with trembling fingers. "Thank you," she whispered. "I don't know what I would do without you."

As Vanessa left, Catherine sat back in her chair, her mind racing. Vanessa's story was troubling, but there was a nagging feeling in the back of her mind that something didn't quite add up. Catherine had seen countless cases of abuse over the years, but this one felt different. There was something about Vanessa that didn't sit right with her.

Catherine had always prided herself on her ability to see through the layers of her clients' stories, to get to the heart of the truth. But Vanessa's case was going to be a challenge. There was more beneath the surface, and Catherine knew she'd have to dig deeper if she wanted to truly understand what was going on.

As she gathered her things to leave the office, Catherine couldn't shake the feeling that Vanessa's story was just the beginning of something much more complicated, something that would test Catherine's own limits in ways she hadn't anticipated.

And for the first time in a long time, Catherine felt a twinge of uncertainty—a rare feeling for a woman who had built her career on being certain about everything. But this case, this woman, would unravel that certainty thread by thread.

Catherine Faber's office, once a sanctuary of healing, had become a stage for deception. The meticulously arranged bookshelves, the framed degrees on the walls, and the comfortable armchairs—every element was a testament to the facade Catherine had carefully crafted. Her rise from a promising psychologist to a celebrated champion of abuse survivors had been meteoric, but beneath the surface, the machinery of manipulation was quietly grinding away.

Vanessa Hale sat across from Catherine, her demeanor a blend of anxious anticipation and controlled composure. The morning sunlight filtered through the blinds, casting faint stripes of light across her designer suit. Vanessa's once-perfect veneer seemed slightly chipped, but she had perfected the art of maintaining appearances. Her eyes, a striking shade of blue, revealed glimpses of the storm within—a storm Catherine was about to fan into a tempest.

Catherine leaned back in her chair, her fingers steepled before her lips. "Vanessa," she began, her voice soft yet imbued with authority, "you've made incredible strides. Your story is powerful, but we need to ensure that every detail resonates with the gravity of your experience. The public needs to understand the full scope of your pain."

Vanessa's gaze flickered with uncertainty, but she nodded slowly. "I want to be honest, Catherine. I've told my story as accurately as I can. Evan's actions—"

"No, no," Catherine interrupted gently. "It's not about honesty per se. It's about making sure the full impact of your experience is conveyed. We need to amplify the emotional weight. The more visceral the portrayal, the stronger the public's reaction will be."

Vanessa's brow furrowed. "I'm not sure what you mean. I've been as truthful as possible. Evan's behavior was abhorrent."

Catherine smiled reassuringly. "I understand, Vanessa. But let's think about how we present your experiences. The more vivid and detailed your recounting, the more it will resonate with the media and the public. You need to make them see—feel—exactly what you went through."

Vanessa hesitated, clearly uncomfortable with the suggestion. "But isn't there a risk of exaggerating? I don't want to mislead anyone."

Catherine's smile remained, but her eyes sharpened with a glint of something calculating. "We're not misleading anyone. We're emphasizing the truth. Your story is a powerful testament to the struggles you faced. We need to ensure it has the impact it deserves."

The conversation shifted as Catherine guided Vanessa through a series of interviews and public appearances, each carefully crafted to portray Vanessa as a victim of unrelenting abuse. Catherine's methods were subtle yet effective; she encouraged Vanessa to recall and elaborate on the more distressing moments of her marriage, suggesting that certain incidents were more harrowing than Vanessa initially described.

Each session left Vanessa feeling increasingly exposed, but Catherine's persuasive rhetoric framed it as a necessary part of their strategy. The interviews became more sensational, the public narrative more gripping. Catherine had a knack for drawing out dramatic details, weaving Vanessa's story into a compelling narrative that played into the media's hunger for scandal.

As Vanessa's story gained traction, Catherine reveled in the growing media attention. Her face was now a fixture on television screens, her voice a staple of news reports. The accolades poured in, lauding her for her groundbreaking work. Yet, Catherine's success was tinged with a creeping unease. The lines between support and manipulation began to blur, her methods veering dangerously close to exploitation.

In private moments, Catherine confronted her reflection in the office mirror, searching for the person she used to be. The image that stared back was not the heroic figure celebrated in the media but a woman who had sacrificed her ethical principles on the altar of fame. The internal conflict was palpable, but she buried it beneath layers of professional detachment.

Meanwhile, Vanessa's growing prominence began to reveal cracks in the façade. The more Catherine pressed for dramatic details, the more Vanessa's story seemed to shift. Small inconsistencies began to emerge—stories that didn't quite add up or details that seemed oddly embellished. Catherine, acutely aware of the potential fallout, worked tirelessly to polish the narrative, dismissing any doubts with a practiced ease.

In her office, Catherine paced restlessly, her mind racing through the implications of each new development. She was acutely aware of the delicate balance she was trying to maintain—the need to protect Vanessa's image while safeguarding her own. Every misstep, every slip, could unravel the carefully constructed narrative that had become both their salvation and their downfall.

As Vanessa's public profile soared, Catherine began to see the tangible benefits of her efforts. High-profile interviews, magazine covers, and glowing testimonials from prominent figures cemented Vanessa's place in the public eye. The media frenzy surrounding the case was unparalleled, and Catherine's role as the guiding force behind Vanessa's transformation into a national symbol of victimhood was undeniable.

But with every success came the mounting pressure to keep up the facade. Catherine's interactions with Vanessa grew more intense, her manipulation more overt. She began to subtly encourage Vanessa to adopt increasingly dramatic and emotional stances in interviews, pushing the boundaries of authenticity. The lines between truth and fabrication became increasingly blurred, driven by Catherine's need to sustain the momentum of their success.

Despite her growing discomfort, Vanessa was swept along by the tide of her newfound fame. The public's adoration, the media's constant attention—it was intoxicating. Catherine's influence over Vanessa became more pronounced, as the socialite found herself increasingly dependent on her psychologist's guidance. The dynamic between them was shifting, with Vanessa becoming a pawn in Catherine's game of professional advancement.

Behind closed doors, Vanessa's anxiety grew. The pressure to maintain the narrative weighed heavily on her. Catherine's insistence on amplifying the story, on pushing for ever more dramatic revelations, left Vanessa feeling increasingly unsettled. She began to question the true nature of her experience and whether the version of her story being portrayed was entirely her own.

Catherine, ever the manipulator, masked her growing unease with a veneer of calm professionalism. She maintained the illusion of control, steering Vanessa's story with a deft hand. The media's voracious appetite for sensationalism played into Catherine's strategy, allowing her to steer the narrative with increasing precision. Vanessa's personal struggles were twisted into a public spectacle, her experiences molded into a compelling, if distorted, tale of abuse.

As the court battle approached, Catherine's involvement in shaping Vanessa's story reached its zenith. The legal strategy she employed was designed to maximize the emotional impact, leveraging every detail of Vanessa's narrative to create a compelling case for the jury. Catherine's expertise in psychological manipulation was evident in the way she had sculpted Vanessa's testimony, ensuring that every emotion was amplified, every distress heightened.

Yet, as the trial loomed, Catherine couldn't shake the nagging sense of impending doom. The more she pushed, the more she realized how fragile their constructed reality had become. The veneer of success began to crack, revealing the underlying instability of their carefully managed facade. Vanessa's increasingly erratic behavior and the inconsistencies in her story were becoming harder to ignore.

In a final, desperate bid to cement their control over the narrative, Catherine orchestrated a series of public appearances designed to bolster Vanessa's image and distract from the growing scrutiny. The media coverage was relentless, and Catherine played her role to perfection, presenting herself as the unwavering advocate for a woman who had suffered unimaginable abuse. But beneath the surface, the cracks were widening, and Catherine's carefully constructed world was on the verge of collapse.

The public's adoration and the media's scrutiny were now inextricably linked to Catherine's success. Her career, built on the fragile foundation of Vanessa's story, was at a critical juncture. As the trial approached, the pressure to maintain the illusion of truth and integrity was immense. Catherine was trapped in a web of her own making, struggling to navigate the complex interplay of manipulation, deception, and self-preservation.

As the courtroom drama unfolded, Catherine's carefully crafted narrative was put to the ultimate test. The stakes were higher than ever, and the consequences of any misstep were potentially catastrophic. Vanessa's story, once a beacon of hope, was now a source of intense scrutiny and danger. Catherine was left to grapple with the consequences of her actions and the harsh reality of the world she had created.

In the end, the carefully constructed narrative that had propelled Catherine and Vanessa to prominence was teetering on the brink of collapse. The illusions of success and control were giving way to the harsh reality of truth and consequence. Catherine's world was unraveling, and the price of her ambition was becoming painfully clear.

Chapter 3: Seeds of Doubt

The sun cast long shadows across the courtroom as Catherine Faber took her seat at the defense table, the air thick with tension. Vanessa Hale, once the epitome of grace and poise, now sat across from her, a shadow of her former self. The case that had once seemed so clear-cut had taken a turn for the worse, and the stakes had never been higher.

Vanessa's testimony had been compelling, a poignant narrative of psychological and physical abuse. But as the days of the trial stretched into weeks, subtle cracks began to form in her story. Evan Hale's defense team was methodical and relentless, scrutinizing every detail of Vanessa's past, peeling back layers to reveal inconsistencies that threatened to undermine her credibility.

Catherine had initially been confident, even cocky. She was the celebrated expert, the hero who had guided Vanessa out of a hellish marriage. The media adored her, the public idolized her, and her career seemed on an unstoppable trajectory. But as Evan Hale's legal team continued their aggressive cross-examinations, cracks in the façade of the case began to appear.

It started with seemingly minor inconsistencies in Vanessa's testimony. Small details that didn't quite align, contradictions that could be dismissed as simple errors. But as the defense team dug deeper, the discrepancies grew larger, more significant. Vanessa's accounts of her husband's behavior were being challenged on multiple fronts. Witnesses who had once supported her claims were now being questioned, their statements examined for signs of collusion or exaggeration.

The courtroom was a stage for a high-stakes drama, each side playing their part with precision. The defense's strategy was clear: if they could cast doubt on Vanessa's credibility, they could dismantle the entire case. They began by attacking her character, suggesting that she had been financially motivated to exaggerate her claims. They presented evidence of Vanessa's lavish lifestyle, casting her as a manipulative opportunist rather than a victim.

The most damaging moment came when Evan Hale's team produced a series of emails and financial records that suggested Vanessa had been planning her departure from the marriage long before the allegations of abuse had surfaced. They argued that her claims were part of a calculated move to secure a favorable divorce settlement and gain public sympathy.

Catherine watched from the defense table, her heart racing. She could see the seeds of doubt taking root in the minds of the jurors. Vanessa, who had once seemed like an unassailable beacon of truth, was now being portrayed as a schemer who had used her trauma as a means to an end. The shift in narrative was unsettling, and Catherine found herself grappling with the implications.

She tried to maintain her composure, to project confidence and certainty. But beneath the surface, she was increasingly anxious. The walls were closing in, and she could feel the pressure mounting. Catherine had invested so much in Vanessa's case, both personally and professionally. The thought of it all unraveling was almost unbearable.

In the quiet moments between court sessions, Catherine wrestled with her thoughts. She replayed Vanessa's testimony in her mind, searching for any indication that the defense might be right. She considered the possibility that Vanessa's story might not be entirely truthful, but she pushed the thought away. After all, she had believed in Vanessa's narrative. She had guided her, supported her, and fought for her. To think that Vanessa might have been lying—or worse, that Catherine might have been complicit in some form of deception—was a notion too painful to entertain.

The days dragged on, and each new revelation from the defense seemed to chip away at the case. Vanessa's once-clear story began to look more like a tangled web of half-truths and embellishments. The media, ever hungry for new angles, seized on the developing drama. Headlines began to question the integrity of Vanessa's claims, and by extension, the credibility of Catherine's methods.

Catherine's phone rang incessantly. Calls from reporters, from colleagues, from friends who were all eager to know how things were going. She found herself dodging questions, offering platitudes that she hoped would buy her time. The pressure was unrelenting, and the fear of what might come next was palpable.

One evening, Catherine found herself alone in her office, surrounded by stacks of case files and legal documents. The room was dimly lit, the only sound the soft hum of her computer and the rustle of papers as she sifted through them. She was trying to piece together a strategy for the next day's proceedings, but her thoughts kept drifting to the mounting evidence against Vanessa.

In a rare moment of introspection, Catherine allowed herself to consider the possibility that she might have been wrong. Had she been so consumed by her own quest for justice that she had failed to see the truth? Had her own unresolved trauma clouded her judgment, causing her to overlook crucial details and inconsistencies?

The thought was unsettling, but Catherine couldn't deny that something was off. She began to review her notes from her sessions with Vanessa, searching for any signs that might have hinted at the discrepancies now being exposed. The more she read, the more she questioned her own role in shaping Vanessa's narrative.

As Catherine dug deeper, she found herself confronting uncomfortable truths. She had always prided herself on her ability to empathize with her clients, to understand their pain and guide them through their darkest moments. But now, she was forced to confront the possibility that her empathy had sometimes crossed into manipulation. Had she, in her quest to help, inadvertently pushed her clients to adopt victim narratives that suited her own agenda?

The lines between advocacy and manipulation were blurring, and Catherine felt increasingly trapped. The case that had once seemed like a clear-cut triumph was now a source of profound uncertainty. With each passing day, the cracks in Vanessa's story grew wider, and Catherine found herself scrambling to maintain control.

The trial continued, and each new revelation from the defense team seemed to shift the ground beneath Catherine's feet. The stakes were higher than ever, and the pressure to defend Vanessa's story—and by extension, her own reputation—was overwhelming. Catherine knew that if she failed, the fallout would be catastrophic, not just for Vanessa, but for her own career and credibility.

In the courtroom, Catherine sat with a facade of calm, but inside, she was a whirlwind of anxiety and doubt. The seed of uncertainty had taken root, and she was now faced with the daunting task of reconciling her belief in Vanessa's story with the growing evidence suggesting otherwise. The cracks were becoming chasms, and Catherine was caught in a perilous game where every move could have dire consequences.

The trial was not just a legal battle; it was a test of Catherine's own moral and professional integrity. The cracks in Vanessa's story were a mirror reflecting the doubts and fears that had long lurked in the shadows of Catherine's own mind. As the days wore on, Catherine faced the harsh reality that the lines between hero and villain, truth and deception, were not as clear as she had once believed.

Catherine Faber's office, once a sanctuary of calm and control, now felt like a cage. The room, adorned with soothing shades of blue and soft lighting, seemed to pulse with an ominous energy that Catherine couldn't shake. The tranquility she had cultivated for years was now a façade, crumbling under the weight of growing doubt and scrutiny.

The day started with a call from her assistant, Emily, who was trying to sound upbeat despite the storm outside. "Dr. Faber, there's a news report you might want to see. It's about Vanessa's case. Apparently, Evan Hale's legal team is questioning the credibility of her allegations."

Catherine's heart skipped a beat. She had anticipated scrutiny but hoped it would be manageable. Vanessa Hale had become the poster child for abused women, and Catherine had made sure of it. Now, though, the storm clouds were gathering faster than she had prepared for.

She flipped on the TV in her office and tuned into the morning news. The screen was filled with a headline that made her stomach churn: "Vanessa Hale's Allegations Under Fire: Questions Raised About Her Credibility". A segment was already running, featuring clips of Evan Hale's attorney, Robert Quinn, fiercely defending his client and hinting at discrepancies in Vanessa's story.

The attorney's words were like daggers. "We've uncovered inconsistencies in Vanessa Hale's statements. What was once presented as a clear-cut case of abuse is now being scrutinized as potentially exaggerated or even fabricated. We believe there's a troubling pattern here, and we're committed to exposing it."

Catherine's mind raced. This was not just about Vanessa anymore; this was about her own reputation. If the defense team succeeded in casting doubt on Vanessa's allegations, it would inevitably cast a shadow on Catherine's methods and, by extension, her career. She knew the media's hunger for scandal would only amplify the situation.

"Dr. Faber?" Emily's voice cut through her thoughts. "Are you okay?"

"Get me the latest updates from the legal team. I need to know exactly what they're saying and what evidence they have," Catherine replied, her voice sharp despite her attempts to remain calm.

The rest of the morning was a whirlwind of meetings and phone calls. Catherine's usual poise was replaced with a sense of urgency and anxiety. Each report, each piece of evidence brought to her by her staff, only fueled her apprehension. The cracks in Vanessa's story were becoming more pronounced, and the media was picking up on them with a fervor.

By noon, Catherine was scheduled to give a press briefing. Her PR team had prepped her with responses to anticipated questions, but no amount of preparation could shield her from the gnawing sense of unease. She arrived at the press conference, her face a mask of professional serenity as she approached the podium.

"Ladies and gentlemen," she began, her voice steady but her mind racing, "I want to address the recent reports regarding Vanessa Hale's case. As you know, my role has always been to support survivors of abuse, and I stand by the integrity of Vanessa's claims."

The room was filled with flashing cameras and probing questions. Catherine fielded each inquiry with practiced ease, but inside, she was a bundle of nerves. The questions were becoming sharper, more critical, and she could sense the growing tide of doubt among the journalists.

"What about the inconsistencies in Vanessa Hale's statements?" one reporter pressed. "How do you respond to the claim that she might have exaggerated or fabricated her abuse?"

Catherine's mind raced for a convincing answer. "It's not uncommon for survivors to struggle with consistency when recounting traumatic experiences," she said, her voice betraying a hint of strain. "Trauma affects memory, and what might seem like inconsistency could be a natural response to such stress."

The reporters scribbled notes and exchanged skeptical glances. Catherine could feel the shifting atmosphere, the realization that her control over the narrative was slipping.

After the briefing, Catherine returned to her office, her head throbbing with the stress of the day. She paced the room, her thoughts tangled in anxiety. Vanessa had always been a fragile figure in her eyes, but now, with the mounting evidence of discrepancies, Catherine wondered if she had misjudged the situation.

She dialed Vanessa's number, her hands trembling slightly. The call went to voicemail. "Vanessa, it's Catherine. We need to talk as soon as possible. Please call me back."

The rest of the day was spent in a haze of legal documents, media reports, and anxious calls to her legal team. Catherine was losing control, and she could feel the pressure of the situation building to a breaking point.

As evening approached, Catherine decided to visit Vanessa in person. She needed answers, needed to gauge the situation directly. Vanessa's upscale apartment building loomed before her, a stark contrast to the turmoil inside Catherine's mind.

She took the elevator to Vanessa's floor, each chime of the elevator bells seeming louder in her ears. When Vanessa opened the door, her usually poised demeanor was replaced with a look of exhaustion and distress.

"Catherine," Vanessa said, her voice barely a whisper. "I didn't know if you'd come."

Catherine stepped inside, her eyes scanning the disheveled apartment. The pristine image of Vanessa's life seemed to have crumbled. "We need to talk," Catherine said firmly. "I'm hearing disturbing things about the case. What's going on?"

Vanessa sank onto the couch, her hands wringing together nervously. "I don't know what to say. There's been so much pressure. I just wanted to get out of that marriage. But now... now it feels like it's all falling apart."

Catherine sat beside her, her mind racing. "Did you exaggerate your story? Did you fabricate any part of it?"

Vanessa looked at her with tear-filled eyes. "I didn't mean to. I was just so desperate to get out. Maybe I did embellish some things. But I thought I was doing what was necessary."

Catherine's heart sank. This was not just about Vanessa's credibility; it was about her own. The realization that Vanessa had not been entirely truthful was a blow, but what stung more was the reflection on Catherine's own role. Had she pushed Vanessa too far? Had her own trauma and drive for success led her to manipulate the situation?

"Vanessa," Catherine said slowly, "I need you to be honest with me. Did I push you into making your story more dramatic than it was?"

Vanessa's gaze fell to the floor. "You believed in me so much. Maybe I wanted to believe it too. But now... I don't know if I can keep this up."

Catherine left Vanessa's apartment with a heavy heart. The weight of the conversation pressed down on her, and she could feel the ground shifting beneath her feet. The stakes were higher than she had ever anticipated, and the echoes of her own unresolved past were coming back to haunt her.

As she drove home, her thoughts were a jumble of self-recrimination and anxiety. The media was relentless, the legal challenges mounting, and now, her own client was questioning the integrity of her story. It was a perfect storm of doubt and scrutiny, and Catherine was at the center, struggling to keep her head above water.

The following days were a blur of legal consultations, media appearances, and sleepless nights. Catherine's once-celebrated methods were under attack, and her own role in the scandal was becoming more apparent. She was facing not only the collapse of her professional reputation but also a deep, personal reckoning with her own motivations and actions.

By the end of the week, the pressure had reached a breaking point. Catherine's therapist, Dr. Collins, had been trying to get in touch with her, sensing that Catherine's carefully maintained facade was cracking. When Catherine finally sat down for her session, Dr. Collins was immediately struck by the depth of her distress.

"Catherine, you're clearly overwhelmed," Dr. Collins said gently. "You're facing intense scrutiny, and it's natural to feel like everything is closing in on you. But you need to take a step back and reassess your situation."

Catherine looked at her therapist, her eyes filled with a mix of fear and anger. "I don't know what's real anymore. I've spent so long convincing others of the truth, and now I'm questioning my own reality."

Dr. Collins nodded sympathetically. "It sounds like you're facing a profound crisis of confidence. You've built your career on helping others, but now you're confronted with the possibility that you might have played a role in manipulating their stories."

The session continued with Catherine exploring her feelings of guilt, doubt, and fear. The conversation was an emotional rollercoaster, forcing Catherine to confront the possibility that her past traumas and her relentless drive for success had led her down a dangerous path.

As she left the session, Catherine felt a mixture of exhaustion and clarity. The path ahead was uncertain, but one thing was becoming painfully clear: she had to face the consequences of her actions, no matter how devastating they might be.

With each passing day, the walls were closing in. The media was relentless, and the legal challenges were mounting. Catherine was caught in a web of her own making, and the only way out was to confront the truth—both about Vanessa's case and about herself.

The struggle was far from over, but Catherine knew one thing for certain: she could no longer hide from the reality of her own actions. The seeds of doubt had been sown, and now it was time to see what they would grow into.

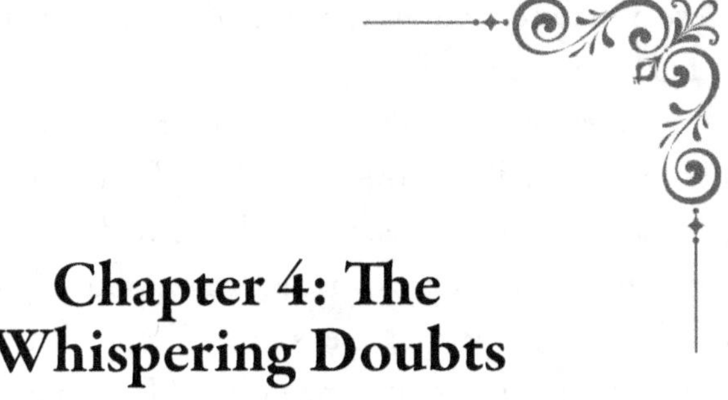

Chapter 4: The Whispering Doubts

The morning light filtered through the blinds of Catherine Faber's office, casting long, narrow shadows across the room. The soft glow illuminated her face, revealing the fatigue that had become a constant companion over the past few weeks. It had been a whirlwind of accusations and scrutiny, and now, as Catherine stared at the stacks of files and media clippings on her desk, she felt a gnawing sense of dread.

The phone rang, slicing through the silence. Catherine picked it up, her hand trembling slightly. It was Karen Albright, one of her former clients. "Dr. Faber, it's urgent. I need to speak with you, and it can't wait."

Catherine's heart sank. Karen was one of several former clients who had recently begun questioning their own experiences, casting doubt on Catherine's methods and suggesting that perhaps her influence had been more profound—and manipulative—than they had initially realized. "Karen, please, come to my office. We need to talk."

Half an hour later, Karen arrived, her demeanor a stark contrast to the composed woman Catherine remembered. Her eyes were red, and she clutched a worn leather handbag as if it were a lifeline. She sat down, and the two women faced each other across the desk.

"Karen, what's going on?" Catherine's voice was steady, but her mind raced with the possibility of what might come next.

Karen took a deep breath. "I've been doing a lot of thinking since all this media frenzy started. I've read some of the things people are saying about you, and I've been questioning my own memories. I thought it was just me—maybe I was just looking for someone to blame for everything that went wrong in my life."

Catherine leaned forward, her gaze fixed on Karen's face. "And what have you concluded?"

Karen hesitated, her fingers nervously tapping the edge of her handbag. "I'm not sure. But I remember you being very insistent about my experiences, about how I should view them. It's like you were guiding me to see things a certain way. At the time, I thought it was just therapy, but now I'm wondering if it was more than that."

Catherine's mind raced. She had always prided herself on her ability to help her clients confront their issues, but if Karen's doubts were valid, it would mean that her reputation—and her career—were in even more peril than she had thought. "Karen, you know I only want what's best for my clients. My methods are based on years of experience and a deep understanding of psychological trauma. Sometimes, people need guidance to see things more clearly."

Karen shook her head. "It wasn't just guidance, Dr. Faber. It felt like you were shaping my narrative. You were pushing me to see myself as a victim, and now I'm wondering if it was really my truth, or if it was what you wanted me to believe."

Before Catherine could respond, Karen stood up, her face pale and her eyes filled with confusion. "I need to think about this more. I just wanted you to know how I feel."

Karen left the office, and Catherine was left alone with her thoughts. The conversation had been unsettling, but it was just the beginning. Karen was not the only one questioning her practices. Other former clients had begun to speak out, each adding a new layer of complexity to the growing scandal.

Later that afternoon, Catherine met with her lawyer, Richard Collins, a sharp-witted man who had been instrumental in helping her navigate the legal intricacies of the current crisis. Richard's office was filled with the scent of freshly brewed coffee and the faint hum of the air conditioning. As he reviewed the documents on his desk, Catherine paced back and forth, her anxiety palpable.

"Richard, I'm getting worried. Clients like Karen are starting to question their experiences with me. What if this turns into a full-blown investigation into my methods?" Catherine's voice was strained.

Richard looked up from the papers, his expression serious. "Catherine, I've been following the developments closely. It's not just Karen—there are other former clients coming forward with similar concerns. We need to address this head-on before it spirals out of control."

Catherine's thoughts raced. She had always believed in the efficacy of her methods, but the mounting criticism and the possibility of legal action were creating a storm that threatened to overwhelm her. "What do we do?"

Richard's gaze was steady. "We need to find out exactly what these clients are saying and whether there's any truth to their claims. If we can demonstrate that your methods were sound and that these clients are misinterpreting their experiences, we might be able to mitigate the damage."

The plan sounded reasonable, but Catherine couldn't shake the feeling that her entire career was on the line. She knew that addressing the concerns of her former clients was crucial, but she also needed to control the narrative and prevent the scandal from gaining further traction.

In the days that followed, Catherine's office was inundated with calls from former clients and the media. The once-celebrated psychologist was now facing a barrage of questions and allegations. As she sifted through the growing pile of documents and media reports, she found herself increasingly isolated. The admiration and respect she had once commanded seemed like a distant memory, replaced by a looming sense of doom.

One afternoon, while reviewing a series of emails from former clients, Catherine came across a particularly troubling message from Emily Thompson, a client who had been very vocal about her experiences during the height of the media frenzy. The email detailed Emily's concerns about how Catherine had handled her case, suggesting that Catherine had pressured her into seeing her past in a more dramatic light than it had actually been.

The message was a harsh reminder of how Catherine's methods were being scrutinized. Emily's doubts echoed Karen's, and the implications were clear: if multiple clients were questioning their experiences, the foundation of Catherine's career was at risk.

Catherine decided she needed to confront the issue head-on. She reached out to Emily, requesting a meeting to discuss her concerns. Emily agreed, and they arranged to meet at a small café in town. The meeting was set for the following day, and Catherine could only hope that the discussion would provide some clarity and a path forward.

As Catherine prepared for the meeting, she couldn't help but reflect on the nature of her work. Had she, in her quest to help her clients, crossed ethical boundaries? Had her own unresolved trauma influenced her approach in ways she hadn't fully acknowledged? The questions were uncomfortable, but they were necessary if she was to understand the full scope of the allegations against her.

The next day, Catherine arrived at the café early, hoping to gather her thoughts before meeting Emily. The café was a cozy, dimly lit space with a calming ambiance, a stark contrast to the turmoil she felt inside. She ordered a coffee and took a seat by the window, waiting for Emily to arrive.

When Emily walked in, her demeanor was guarded. She sat down across from Catherine, her eyes wary but resolute. "Dr. Faber, thank you for meeting with me."

Catherine forced a smile, trying to convey sincerity. "Emily, I appreciate you taking the time to talk. I've been reviewing your email and want to understand your concerns better."

Emily nodded, her gaze steady. "I've been thinking a lot about our sessions and the way you framed my experiences. At first, I thought you were helping me, but now I wonder if you were pushing me to see things through a specific lens. I started questioning whether my memories were really as vivid as I thought."

Catherine felt a pang of anxiety. "Emily, I want to assure you that my intention was always to help you, not to manipulate you. Sometimes, therapy involves guiding clients to confront difficult truths, but I never intended to shape your experiences in a way that wasn't authentic."

Emily's expression softened, but there was a hint of skepticism in her eyes. "I understand that therapy can be complex, but I feel like my narrative was influenced. I just want to know if I was misled or if I misunderstood."

Catherine listened carefully, her mind racing as she tried to reconcile Emily's concerns with her own understanding of her methods. "Emily, if there were any ways in which my approach might have affected your perceptions, I want to address that. My goal is always to support and empower my clients."

The conversation continued, with Catherine and Emily delving into the details of their sessions. As they spoke, Catherine found herself grappling with the possibility that her well-intentioned methods might have been flawed. The meeting ended with no clear resolution, but Catherine knew that the road ahead would be challenging.

As she left the café, Catherine felt a profound sense of unease. The doubts and accusations surrounding her work were intensifying, and the path to restoring her reputation seemed increasingly uncertain. She knew that she needed to confront the issues head-on and find a way to address the concerns of her former clients, but the weight of the scrutiny was overwhelming.

The days that followed were marked by a growing sense of urgency. Catherine continued to meet with former clients and respond to media inquiries, all while trying to maintain her professional composure. The allegations against her were taking a toll on her mental health, and the pressure to prove her innocence was mounting.

In the midst of the chaos, Catherine found herself reflecting on her career and the choices that had led her to this point. She had always been driven by a desire to help others, but now she was faced with the harsh reality that her methods—and her intentions—were being questioned. The journey to rebuild her reputation would be arduous, and Catherine knew that the road ahead was fraught with challenges.

As the weeks progressed, the scandal continued to unfold, with former clients coming forward and media coverage intensifying.

Catherine Faber had spent the last week navigating through a storm of mounting criticism. Her once-celebrated reputation was now under siege, each day unveiling new cracks in the facade of her success. Her office, once a sanctuary of triumph, now felt like a prison. The walls, adorned with accolades and framed newspaper clippings of her celebrated victories, seemed to close in on her.

The scent of freshly brewed coffee was lost on Catherine as she stared at her computer screen. Headlines flashed across her newsfeed, each more damning than the last: "Vanessa Hale: A Victim or a Fraud?"; "The Psychologist Who Manipulated the Truth?"; "Catherine Faber Under Scrutiny: How Deep Does the Deception Go?" The articles were relentless, each piece of evidence more damning, further chipping away at her carefully constructed world.

But it wasn't just the media that troubled Catherine. Vanessa Hale, the socialite whose case had catapulted Catherine into the limelight, was starting to hint at inconsistencies in her own story. What had once been a clear narrative of abuse was now becoming a muddled mess, and Catherine found herself on the defensive.

The day began with a call from Vanessa. Catherine hesitated before picking up the phone. Vanessa's voice, usually smooth and controlled, was now tinged with a nervous edge.

"Catherine, we need to talk," Vanessa said, her tone brooking no argument.

Catherine agreed to meet at a quiet café, a neutral ground where they could talk away from prying eyes. As Catherine arrived, she found Vanessa already seated at a corner table, her demeanor tight and guarded. The once glamorous woman now seemed fragile, her designer dress hanging on her like a borrowed piece of clothing.

"What's going on, Vanessa?" Catherine asked as she sat down, trying to keep her voice calm and professional.

Vanessa took a deep breath, her eyes darting around as if she feared someone might overhear. "I've been thinking... about everything that's happened."

Catherine's heart skipped a beat. "Go on."

"I've started to wonder if maybe I exaggerated some things. I mean, it's not that I'm saying everything was a lie, but... I might have made it sound worse than it actually was."

Catherine's stomach twisted. "Why are you telling me this now? You've already made your statements. We've been through so much together."

Vanessa's face was a mask of guilt and fear. "I don't know, Catherine. It's just... the pressure. The media. The case. It's all starting to feel... overwhelming."

Catherine's mind raced. This was not just about Vanessa's shifting story; it was a potential nightmare for Catherine's entire career. "What do you want to do?" she asked carefully.

"I don't know," Vanessa admitted, her voice trembling. "Maybe we should... just let things lie. I'm scared of what might happen if people find out."

Catherine felt a surge of panic. Vanessa's wavering confidence could unravel the entire narrative Catherine had carefully crafted. "We need to stay strong," Catherine said, her voice firm but laced with desperation. "We can't let them see any weakness."

Vanessa's eyes were pleading. "But if the truth comes out... if people realize I wasn't as much of a victim as we said, what happens to us?"

Catherine tried to steady her racing thoughts. Vanessa was no longer the untouchable socialite; she was a frightened woman who had become a liability. "We'll deal with it," Catherine said, trying to sound reassuring. "But you need to stay committed. No more doubts."

As Vanessa nodded reluctantly, Catherine's mind spun with possible solutions. The media was already beginning to question Vanessa's claims, and now, with Vanessa herself hinting at inconsistencies, the situation was rapidly spiraling out of control.

Later that day, Catherine met with her lawyer, Linda, in a dimly lit conference room. Linda's expression was grim as Catherine relayed the details of her conversation with Vanessa.

"This is a mess," Linda said, rubbing her temples. "Vanessa's wavering could be disastrous for us. The media will have a field day."

Catherine clenched her fists. "We need to find a way to control the narrative. We can't let this destroy everything we've worked for."

Linda's eyes were sharp. "We should consider a strategy. Maybe we can discredit the doubters, strengthen Vanessa's original claims, or find a way to discredit any emerging allegations."

Catherine nodded, her mind racing. "We need to be proactive. We can't afford to wait and see what happens. We need to act now."

The next few days were a blur of frantic phone calls, meetings, and strategizing. Catherine threw herself into damage control, focusing on publicly defending Vanessa's story and attempting to discredit the claims of those questioning her methods. Yet, every attempt to fortify her position seemed to backfire, further fueling the media frenzy.

At home, Catherine's mind was a constant whirl of anxiety. Her nights were filled with restless sleep, haunted by dreams of her own past—of her father's harsh words, the echoes of her mother's sobs, and the suffocating feeling of being trapped. The more she tried to project strength and confidence to the outside world, the more she felt herself crumbling from within.

The breaking point came when a former client, Rachel, publicly accused Catherine of manipulation. Rachel's claims were specific and damning: she alleged that Catherine had convinced her that her past experiences were more traumatic than she initially believed, manipulating her memories to fit a narrative that would benefit Catherine's career.

Rachel's accusations were detailed and chilling. She recounted sessions with Catherine where the psychologist had pushed her to delve deeper into her trauma, guiding her to frame her experiences in a way that would support Catherine's public image. The media seized on Rachel's story, using it as further evidence of Catherine's alleged misconduct.

Catherine's attempts to defend herself only seemed to make matters worse. The media storm grew more intense, with each new revelation pushing her closer to the edge. Her once solid reputation was now shattered, and she was left grappling with the realization that her carefully constructed world was unraveling.

One night, as Catherine sat alone in her office, the weight of her situation pressed down on her. The office, once a symbol of her success, now felt like a tomb. The framed accolades on the walls seemed mocking, reminders of a past that had come crashing down.

As she stared at her reflection in the darkened window, Catherine felt the crushing weight of her own failures. Her career, her carefully curated image, and her sense of purpose were all slipping away. She had fought so hard to build a life dedicated to helping others, only to find herself entangled in the very issues she had sought to combat.

The phone rang, jolting Catherine from her thoughts. It was Linda, her voice tense and urgent.

"Catherine, you need to see this," Linda said. "Vanessa's starting to talk more openly about her doubts. There are reports that she might be ready to make a public statement."

Catherine's heart raced. This was the last thing she needed. "What's she saying?"

"She's suggesting that her story might not have been entirely accurate," Linda said, her voice tight with frustration. "We need to act quickly to address this before it gets worse."

Catherine's mind raced as she considered her options. Vanessa's shifting narrative could destroy what little credibility she had left. She needed to regain control of the situation before it spiraled completely out of her reach.

As Catherine hung up the phone, she realized that her life had become a high-stakes game of survival. Every move she made now carried the risk of further exposing her vulnerabilities and potentially unraveling her entire world. The fight to protect her career and reputation was no longer just about defending her methods—it was about preserving her very sense of self.

In the days that followed, Catherine threw herself into a desperate battle to regain control of the narrative. She appeared on talk shows, gave interviews, and made public statements, all in an attempt to salvage her reputation and refute the mounting accusations. Despite her efforts, the media continued to scrutinize her every move, and public opinion remained divided.

Vanessa's changing story and the revelations from former clients had created a perfect storm of doubt and controversy. Catherine found herself trapped in a web of her own making, struggling to navigate the treacherous waters of public opinion and legal scrutiny.

As Catherine faced the mounting pressure, she began to question her own decisions and motivations. The veneer of control she had maintained for so long was starting to crack, revealing the underlying fears and insecurities that had driven her actions.

The once-unshakeable confidence that had propelled Catherine to success now seemed like a distant memory. The realization that her career—and perhaps her entire identity—was at stake forced her to confront the harsh truth of her own actions and their consequences.

The chapter closed with Catherine standing alone in her office, the weight of her situation bearing down on her. The once-familiar surroundings now felt alien, and the accolades on the walls seemed like cruel reminders of a past that had slipped beyond her grasp.

Chapter 5: Media Frenzy

Catherine Faber had always thrived on control. In her field, it was not just a professional trait but a necessity. Every client she took on was meticulously managed, their stories sculpted to fit into a narrative that served not only their needs but her own reputation. However, nothing had prepared her for the chaos that unfolded when the media spotlight, once her most loyal ally, began to turn against her.

It started subtly, with whispers in the corners of newspapers and online forums. At first, they were just murmurings, faint and disjointed. But as more evidence of Vanessa Hale's inconsistencies surfaced, those whispers grew louder, more insistent. Catherine's name, once synonymous with success, became a target for journalists hungry for a scandal.

It began with a small article in the New York Post. The headline screamed: "Psychologist in Scandal: Did Catherine Faber Push Her Clients Too Far?" The piece was filled with quotes from former clients—those who had started to question their own memories and, by extension, Catherine's role in shaping them. They claimed she had manipulated their perceptions of their abuse, guiding them to adopt the victim narrative she so fervently championed. The article was a firestarter, igniting a blaze of media scrutiny that Catherine had never anticipated.

As the days went by, the coverage only intensified. Major news outlets picked up the story, each one adding its own layer of sensationalism. The media frenzy was relentless, with Catherine's image shifting from revered advocate to a figure of scorn. The public's perception of her as a selfless champion of abuse survivors was being dismantled piece by piece, replaced with the image of a manipulative opportunist.

Catherine's phone rang incessantly. Each call was a potential disaster, a new revelation that threatened to undermine her credibility further. The voicemail inbox was a cacophony of messages from journalists, former clients, and curious acquaintances, each seeking a comment, a soundbite, or even a personal confession. Her public relations team worked tirelessly, trying to manage the damage, but the scale of the crisis was overwhelming.

In her spacious, tastefully decorated office—a sanctuary she had once considered impenetrable—Catherine felt a creeping sense of dread. The room, which had been a symbol of her success, now felt like a cage. The walls seemed to close in on her as she read through the latest headlines. The room was filled with the hum of her assistant, who was sorting through press clippings and coordinating with the PR team. Catherine barely registered the noise, her attention consumed by the growing pile of media reports.

Her anxiety was palpable. The media's portrayal of her as a manipulative fraud was not just damaging her career; it was threatening her entire identity. Catherine had spent years crafting a public persona built on trust and compassion. The thought of that persona being dismantled was both terrifying and maddening. She had to fight back. She had to prove her innocence, restore her reputation, and regain control of the narrative.

The first step in her counter-offensive was a carefully orchestrated press conference. She had planned every detail meticulously, from the carefully selected venue to the carefully crafted statements. She would address the accusations head-on, refute the claims with logic and evidence, and reaffirm her commitment to her clients and her profession.

As she stood before the gathered journalists, her hands gripping the podium, she tried to project an image of confidence. The cameras flashed, and the room was filled with the buzz of anticipation. Catherine took a deep breath and began her statement.

"Ladies and gentlemen, thank you for coming today. I want to address the recent allegations with complete transparency. I understand that the claims made against me are serious, and I want to set the record straight."

She spoke with practiced calm, outlining her commitment to ethical practices and the extensive safeguards she had in place to ensure the well-being of her clients. She detailed the rigorous protocols she followed, the training her staff received, and the numerous positive testimonials she had amassed over the years. Catherine's voice, though steady, carried an undertone of frustration. She was aware that words alone might not be enough to dispel the swirling storm of public opinion.

Despite her well-rehearsed responses, the questions from the press were sharp and probing. Reporters were relentless, digging into her methods, her past cases, and even her personal life. They were not just interested in the facts; they wanted drama, conflict, and scandal. Catherine answered as best as she could, but the more she spoke, the more she felt the weight of the media's scrutiny bearing down on her.

The press conference did little to quell the media storm. If anything, it seemed to intensify it. The headlines the next day were even more damning. Words like "crumbling facade" and "manipulative tactics" dominated the pages. It was clear that the media had seized upon a narrative that painted Catherine as a villain, and they were not going to let go easily.

Catherine tried to find solace in her work, immersing herself in her remaining cases, hoping that focusing on her clients would help her forget the growing turmoil. But it was a futile attempt. Every client meeting was overshadowed by the media's relentless pursuit. Clients who had once trusted her were now questioning her motives, and her ability to help them seemed compromised by the growing public scandal.

As she struggled to maintain her professional composure, Catherine also had to deal with the personal fallout. Friends and colleagues began to distance themselves, wary of being associated with the controversy. Even those who had once been her staunchest supporters seemed hesitant to offer support, their silence a stark reminder of how quickly allegiances could shift.

One evening, after a particularly grueling day of media appearances and client meetings, Catherine sat alone in her office, staring at the framed accolades on her wall. The awards, certificates, and newspaper clippings that had once celebrated her achievements now seemed to mock her. The very symbols of her success had become relics of a past that seemed increasingly distant and irrelevant.

Her thoughts were interrupted by a knock on the door. It was her assistant, bearing the latest batch of press clippings and a new wave of voicemails. Catherine took the materials with a resigned sigh, her eyes scanning the headlines once more. The media frenzy had reached a fever pitch, and she knew that turning the tide would be a monumental task.

In the days that followed, Catherine's life became a series of high-stakes battles. She was determined to clear her name, but each step forward seemed to be met with new challenges. The media's portrayal of her as a manipulative fraud had taken on a life of its own, and reversing the damage seemed almost impossible.

She continued to work with her PR team, strategizing on ways to counteract the negative press. They planned interviews with trusted news outlets, prepared detailed responses to the allegations, and sought to present Catherine in a more favorable light. But as the scandal deepened, even these efforts felt like they were having little effect. The media had already made up its mind, and the public's perception was shifting faster than Catherine could manage.

The pressure mounted, and Catherine found herself increasingly isolated. Her once-bustling office now felt empty, the silence a stark contrast to the noise and chaos that had consumed her life. She was left to confront the harsh reality that her carefully crafted image was unraveling, and the more she tried to grasp control, the more it seemed to slip through her fingers.

In the midst of the turmoil, Catherine received a visit from an unexpected source. It was a former client, one of the many who had begun to question their memories and the role Catherine had played in shaping their perceptions. The client's visit was a stark reminder of the personal cost of the scandal, and it was clear that Catherine's efforts to salvage her reputation were far from over.

As she faced the reality of her situation, Catherine struggled to reconcile the disparity between the public's perception and her own view of herself. She had dedicated her life to helping others, but now she was being portrayed as the very thing she had spent years fighting against. The media frenzy was not just a professional setback; it was a personal crisis, one that challenged her very sense of identity and purpose.

In the end, Catherine realized that the media's portrayal of her was more than just a series of headlines—it was a reflection of deeper truths about her own life and career. The public's turn against her was a manifestation of the unresolved issues that had haunted her for years, and as she grappled with the fallout, she was forced to confront the complexities of her own motivations and actions.

The media frenzy had only just begun, and Catherine knew that the road ahead would be fraught with challenges. As she prepared for the next phase of her battle, she was acutely aware that the fight to reclaim her reputation was not just about defending her professional achievements; it was about confronting the personal demons that had fueled her rise and, ultimately, her fall.

The phone's persistent ringing sliced through the oppressive silence of Catherine's office, an unsettling reminder of the turmoil now consuming her life. Each ring seemed to echo the clamor outside, where the media's feeding frenzy had reached a fever pitch. Catherine, with her meticulously curated reputation in tatters, could no longer find solace in her once-thriving career. The walls of her sanctuary, lined with accolades and awards, now felt like a prison, each frame a taunting reminder of her fall from grace.

She finally answered the call, her voice strained and hollow. "Catherine Faber."

"Dr. Faber, it's Judith from WEN News," came the voice on the other end, clipped and urgent. "We need a statement regarding the latest allegations. Your silence is only fueling speculation. Our viewers want answers."

Catherine inhaled sharply, her mind racing to construct a response that would stave off the encroaching storm. "I'm not prepared to make a statement at this moment," she replied, trying to sound calm. "I need time to assess the situation."

Judith's voice hardened. "Dr. Faber, your time is running out. The public and the media are growing impatient. You need to address these claims directly."

The line went dead before Catherine could respond. She set the phone down and stared at the swirling mass of headlines on her computer screen, each one a dagger to her already wounded pride. The media had turned against her with a ferocity she had not anticipated. Once hailed as a savior, she was now a pariah, her methods and ethics under relentless scrutiny.

The news was everywhere: "Heroic Psychologist or Manipulative Fraud?" "Catherine Faber's Controversial Methods Exposed!" Each headline was more damning than the last, painting her as a villain in a scandal that had taken on a life of its own.

Catherine had always known the risks of being in the public eye, but she had never imagined this. The careful balance she had maintained between her professional facade and personal demons was unraveling, leaving her exposed and vulnerable. Her mind flitted back to the whispers and doubts that had begun to surface—a creeping realization that her past methods might not have been as flawless as she had once believed.

In her desperation, Catherine called an emergency meeting with her legal team. The firm she had always trusted now seemed distant, their faces clouded with concern and disapproval. Her lead attorney, Mark Bennett, a seasoned litigator known for his steely demeanor, looked over the latest pile of evidence with a grave expression.

"We need to address this head-on," Mark said, his voice steady but tinged with a hint of frustration. "The media's narrative is turning against you, and the allegations are serious. We can't afford to ignore them."

Catherine's fingers drummed nervously on the table. "I need to control the narrative," she said, her voice trembling. "I can't let them paint me as a monster."

Mark raised an eyebrow. "Controlling the narrative is easier said than done. We need to counter these claims with concrete evidence and statements that can discredit the accusations. We need to focus on Vanessa's credibility and, more importantly, address the questions about your own practices."

Catherine nodded, her thoughts a whirlwind of anxiety. "What about the former clients? They're coming out of the woodwork, saying that I manipulated them. What can we do about that?"

"First, we need to verify their claims," Mark said. "We need to gather evidence to either support or refute these allegations. But we also need to prepare for the worst—these claims could be used against you in court."

The weight of Mark's words pressed heavily on Catherine. She had always prided herself on her ability to navigate the complexities of human behavior, but now she was facing a storm of her own making. The public's perception of her, once a pillar of strength and empathy, was now fractured beyond recognition.

As the days passed, Catherine's life became a blur of meetings, legal consultations, and increasingly frantic attempts to salvage her reputation. Each press conference, each statement she made seemed to fall short, failing to stem the tide of negative press. The media's scrutiny was relentless, and the public's fascination with the scandal only seemed to grow.

The accusations against her were damning, but the real threat came from the way they were being amplified. Social media was awash with speculation and condemnation. Twitter threads dissected her every move, Facebook posts called for her to be stripped of her license, and every news outlet seemed eager to add fuel to the fire.

Desperate for a solution, Catherine turned to her closest confidants—her former colleagues, mentors, and friends. She reached out to them for support and advice, hoping they could offer insights or solutions. But their responses were mixed, ranging from cautious support to outright distancing themselves from her.

Dr. Angela Marston, a longtime colleague and friend, was one of the few who offered any form of solace. "Catherine, you need to take a step back," Angela advised. "The media circus is not going to help you. You need to focus on addressing these issues head-on and regaining control over your narrative."

"I'm trying," Catherine said, her voice breaking. "But every time I try to set the record straight, it feels like I'm digging a deeper hole."

Angela's voice softened. "You've built a career on helping others. Don't let this crisis define you. You need to find a way to confront this head-on, not just for your sake but for the sake of those who still believe in you."

Catherine's desperation was mounting. Her once-clear path was now obscured by the chaos of her own making. She knew she had to act quickly to address the growing doubts and accusations, but she was also grappling with her own internal struggle.

Every night, she lay awake, haunted by memories of her father's cruelty and the unspoken fears that had driven her to become the very thing she had once despised. The echoes of her past seemed to blur with the present, creating a disorienting haze that made it difficult to distinguish reality from illusion.

One particularly restless night, Catherine found herself sifting through old case files and client records, searching for anything that could help her counter the allegations. She reviewed notes, transcripts, and therapy session summaries, hoping to find something—anything—that could disprove the claims against her.

In the dim light of her office, she stumbled upon an old file marked "Confidential." It contained detailed notes on one of her early cases, a high-profile client whose allegations of abuse had been instrumental in her rise to prominence. As she read through the file, she found herself grappling with an unsettling realization.

The notes, though meticulously documented, revealed a pattern of behavior that she had overlooked. There were subtle hints of manipulation, moments where her guidance may have influenced the client's perception of their experiences. It was as if she had unconsciously steered them toward a narrative that aligned with her own beliefs and biases.

The realization struck her with the force of a sledgehammer. The lines between her professional guidance and personal convictions had blurred in ways she had never fully acknowledged. The very methods she had once defended with conviction now appeared questionable, if not unethical.

The weight of her findings pressed heavily on Catherine. She knew she had to confront these revelations, but she was paralyzed by fear and uncertainty. The implications of her discoveries threatened to unravel the last vestiges of her credibility and self-worth.

In the midst of her turmoil, Vanessa Hale's voice pierced through her thoughts. Vanessa had called Catherine earlier that day, demanding to speak with her immediately. Catherine, already on edge, had agreed to meet, hoping to find some resolution.

The meeting took place in a secluded café, a stark contrast to the chaos that surrounded Catherine's life. Vanessa, once the epitome of a troubled victim, now exuded a calculated calm. She was dressed impeccably, her demeanor composed and controlled.

"Catherine," Vanessa said, her voice cold but measured. "I need to know where we stand. The media is tearing both of us apart. I need to understand what's going to happen next."

Catherine felt a pang of frustration. "Vanessa, I'm doing everything I can to defend us, but the situation is spiraling out of control. I need your support to counter these claims, but you're not helping with your silence."

Vanessa's eyes narrowed. "I'm trying to protect myself, Catherine. If this gets any worse, it's not just my reputation on the line. You need to make sure that our story doesn't crumble."

Catherine's desperation reached its peak. She had invested so much in defending Vanessa's story that she could no longer see a way out. "I need you to be honest with me, Vanessa. If there's anything you're hiding, now is the time to come clean. The truth will come out eventually, and it could destroy us both."

Vanessa's expression remained impassive. "I've been honest. But you need to understand that the stakes are high. We're both at risk here. If you can't fix this, we're both going to fall."

The conversation left Catherine feeling more isolated than ever. Vanessa's cold detachment and calculated demeanor only heightened her anxiety. The realization that her once-trusted client might be as complicit in the deception as she was gnawed at her.

As the days turned into weeks, Catherine's desperation deepened. She clung to the hope that a strategic move could salvage her reputation and salvage her career. She engaged in frantic consultations with her legal team, drafted carefully worded statements, and attempted to reach out to media contacts.

Despite her efforts, the media continued to scrutinize her every move. The public's fascination with

Chapter 6: The Defense Strikes Back

Catherine Faber sat in her office, her fingers tracing the smooth curve of her pen as she read the latest media headline on her computer screen: "Evan Hale Strikes Back: New Evidence May Prove Vanessa Hale Lied." Her stomach clenched, the tension that had been gnawing at her for weeks now feeling like it had become a permanent resident in her gut.

The headline wasn't just clickbait. She knew that Evan Hale's legal team had been meticulously digging into Vanessa's story. What had once seemed like a slam-dunk case of psychological and physical abuse now had cracks running through it. But Catherine had refused to admit those fractures aloud, even to herself.

She clicked the tab, pulling up the article, scanning for any clues that might hint at what was coming. Evan Hale's lawyer, Roger Whitman, was described as relentless and detail-oriented, his reputation built on dismantling cases just like this one. What worried Catherine most, however, was the mention of a "key piece of evidence" that Evan's team had obtained. The article didn't reveal much more, leaving her in a cold sweat of dread. She knew she needed to prepare, but for what, she wasn't sure.

Two days later, she sat in the back row of the courtroom, Vanessa beside her, twirling a strand of perfectly coiffed hair between her fingers. They were both waiting for the pre-trial hearing to begin. Evan Hale's legal team had requested an emergency hearing to present new evidence. The room was filled with low whispers, reporters shifting in their seats as they prepared for the next big story. Catherine felt the weight of a dozen eyes on her, wondering if they saw her discomfort, wondering if they could sense the anxiety she worked so hard to bury beneath a calm exterior.

Roger Whitman approached the judge's bench with his usual swagger, exuding the confidence of a man who knew he was about to deliver a knockout punch. He placed a thick manila envelope in front of the judge, his voice low but steady as he began to speak.

"Your Honor, I would like to introduce new evidence that proves the defendant, Vanessa Hale, has fabricated significant portions of her abuse claims against my client."

The courtroom buzzed with sudden electricity. Catherine glanced sideways at Vanessa, who sat stiffly, her face betraying no emotion. But Catherine felt the storm brewing. For weeks, Vanessa had grown distant, dodging her calls and showing up late for meetings. Now, it was clear why.

"What is this?" Catherine whispered under her breath, but Vanessa didn't answer.

The evidence, as it turned out, was damning.

Roger Whitman played a series of voicemails, the echoing, familiar sound of Vanessa's voice filling the courtroom. In the messages, Vanessa laughed and joked with a friend, recounting a drunken weekend in the Bahamas, just weeks before the alleged abuse had supposedly begun. More critically, Vanessa's friend questioned the authenticity of her claims against Evan, to which Vanessa replied, "Oh please, it's not that bad. But if I play my cards right, I can make sure it's worth it in the end."

Catherine's breath caught in her throat as the audio played. She had always been skilled at controlling her expressions, but now, she feared her mask was cracking. She could feel the eyes of the courtroom, the scrutiny of the reporters, the whispers of disbelief and judgment.

As the voicemails ended, Roger Whitman stepped back, smug satisfaction painted across his face. The damage had been done. And Catherine knew, deep down, that it wasn't over. They would keep digging. This was just the beginning of Evan Hale's counterattack.

Hours later, back in her office, Catherine sat in silence. Vanessa's parting words echoed in her mind, cold and detached: "I never said it was perfect, Catherine. But it doesn't matter if it's all true. What matters is the narrative you helped me build."

The realization crashed into her like a tidal wave. Vanessa had never truly been her client—she had been her accomplice, a willing participant in the story Catherine had crafted so carefully. And now, that story was beginning to unravel.

Catherine's fingers trembled as she pulled open the file on her desk. In the beginning, she had believed Vanessa's story. Every detail, every tearful confession had fit so perfectly into the pattern she recognized, the pattern that had haunted her since childhood. But now, in the cold light of scrutiny, she could see it for what it was: a manipulation.

She had shaped Vanessa's narrative because she needed it to be true. Just like she had shaped the narratives of so many of her clients. She had seen abuse in places where it didn't always exist, projecting her own pain and trauma onto the lives of the women who came to her for help.

A knock on the door snapped her out of her thoughts. Marissa, her assistant, poked her head in, her expression hesitant.

"Catherine, I think you need to see this."

Marissa handed her a copy of the lawsuit that had just been filed against her. Evan Hale was suing her for defamation, accusing her of manipulating his wife into fabricating the abuse allegations that had destroyed his reputation. Worse still, the lawsuit wasn't just targeting Vanessa's case—it was questioning all of Catherine's previous work, painting her as a reckless psychologist who projected her unresolved trauma onto her clients, coercing them into false memories.

The lawsuit was the first of what she knew would be many.

That night, Catherine sat alone in her apartment, staring out the window at the darkened city below. The weight of her mistakes pressed down on her like a heavy blanket. The lines between right and wrong, victim and perpetrator, had become so blurred in her mind that she wasn't sure where she stood anymore. She had started her career with noble intentions, a deep desire to help women like her mother—women who had suffered in silence, trapped in the webs of their abusers. But somewhere along the way, that mission had become distorted.

She had wanted to be a savior. But now, she was being cast as the villain.

Her phone buzzed on the table beside her, the screen lighting up with an incoming call. It was Vanessa.

For a moment, Catherine considered not answering. But then, with a deep breath, she picked it up.

"Catherine," Vanessa's voice came through the line, cool and composed. "We need to talk."

The next morning, Catherine met Vanessa at a small café on the outskirts of the city, far from the prying eyes of reporters and the public. Vanessa was already seated when she arrived, a steaming cup of coffee in front of her.

"Are you going to tell me what this is really about?" Catherine asked, her voice sharp, cutting through the pretense of pleasantries.

Vanessa took a sip of her coffee, her eyes never leaving Catherine's. "I told you, I never lied completely. Evan was abusive in his own way—controlling, manipulative. But I didn't need you to push me into making it worse than it was. You wanted me to. You needed a story, Catherine. And I gave you one."

Catherine felt her stomach churn. She had always prided herself on being able to read people, to understand their motivations, their fears. But with Vanessa, she had been blind. She had seen what she wanted to see, and now it was all falling apart.

"You knew," Catherine said, her voice barely above a whisper. "You knew I would shape the story the way I did. And you went along with it."

Vanessa smiled, but there was no warmth in it. "Of course I did. It was mutually beneficial, wasn't it? I got out of my marriage, and you got another victory under your belt. Until now."

Catherine sat back in her chair, the enormity of her situation settling in. Vanessa had played her from the start. And now, there was no way out.

By the time Catherine returned to her office, her mind was spinning. Vanessa's words replayed over and over in her head, each repetition cutting deeper than the last.

The lawsuit, the voicemails, Vanessa's betrayal—it was all coming together to paint a picture of her as the manipulator, the villain of the story. And for the first time, Catherine wasn't sure if they were wrong.

Catherine sat at the edge of her office chair, her fingers gripping the armrests so tightly that her knuckles had turned white. The walls, lined with the numerous accolades and awards she'd accumulated over the years, now felt like they were closing in on her. Each framed certificate was a reminder of the reputation she had so carefully constructed—and which now threatened to crumble in the wake of the impending legal disaster.

Her phone vibrated on the desk. The caller ID displayed "Daniel Heller," her attorney. She hesitated before picking up, knowing what the call would bring.

"Daniel," she breathed, trying to steady her voice.

His tone was professional, but the underlying tension was palpable. "Catherine, I won't sugarcoat this. Evan Hale's legal team just filed a lawsuit against you for professional malpractice. They're accusing you of manipulating Vanessa's testimony, coercing her into fabricating the abuse claims. This is serious."

Her stomach dropped. This was the moment she had feared, the point at which her entire world teetered on the edge of destruction. "I didn't coerce her," Catherine said, her voice barely above a whisper, more to convince herself than her attorney.

"You need to prepare for what's coming. The media is going to be all over this, and Evan's team is ready to go after everything—your methods, your ethics, even your credibility as a psychologist."

Catherine's pulse quickened. "But Vanessa's story was real. It had to be real." She could feel the cracks in her own conviction, like a fissure running through her mind. Could it be possible that she had, in her desperation to see justice done, nudged Vanessa in the wrong direction?

"Whether her story was real or not is irrelevant at this point," Daniel replied. "What matters is that they have enough to cast doubt on your methods. I need you to come into the office tomorrow so we can prepare your defense. This won't be easy."

As Catherine ended the call, she stared at the walls of her office once more. Every award, every client success story, now felt like a hollow reminder of what she had built—and what she could lose. Her thoughts drifted back to Vanessa, remembering every meeting, every session where she had pushed Vanessa to confront the memories of abuse. Had she gone too far?

The lawsuit was only the beginning. Evan Hale's legal team was known for their ruthlessness, and they were about to unleash a storm.

Later that evening, Catherine sat in her living room, her laptop open as she scanned through the endless barrage of news articles about the case. The headlines were shifting. Just days ago, they had lauded her as a savior, a hero for women trapped in abusive relationships. Now, the headlines painted her in an entirely different light:

"Psychologist Accused of Manipulating High-Profile Abuse Case"

"Vanessa Hale's Story Crumbling—Did Catherine Faber Coerce Her Client?"

"Evan Hale Strikes Back: Lawsuit Filed Against Famed Psychologist"

Each article seemed to chip away at her confidence, each line of text a hammer blow to the life she had built. The comments sections were even worse, filled with anonymous vitriol from people who once praised her.

She closed the laptop, unable to stomach any more. For the first time in years, Catherine felt something unfamiliar—fear. Real, paralyzing fear that she was about to lose everything. Not just her career, but her identity.

The doorbell rang, pulling her out of her thoughts. She wasn't expecting anyone. Cautiously, she approached the door and peeked through the peephole. To her surprise, standing on the other side was Vanessa Hale.

Catherine hesitated, her mind racing. What was Vanessa doing here? Was this another one of her manipulations? Or was she here to set things right?

With a deep breath, Catherine opened the door.

Vanessa looked worn, her usual polished appearance disheveled. Her eyes darted nervously, as if she were afraid of being seen.

"Can I come in?" Vanessa asked, her voice small.

Catherine stepped aside, allowing her in. Vanessa walked into the living room, pausing to look around at the pristine decor before turning to face Catherine.

"I didn't know where else to go," Vanessa admitted, her voice cracking. "The press... they're everywhere. My life is falling apart."

Catherine couldn't help but feel a pang of sympathy for Vanessa, despite everything. "You're not alone," she said softly, gesturing for Vanessa to sit down. "We'll get through this."

Vanessa shook her head, her hands trembling in her lap. "No, Catherine. You don't understand. It's not just about the lawsuit. They're going to find out everything."

Catherine froze. "What do you mean?"

Vanessa's eyes filled with tears. "I lied, Catherine. I lied about some of the things I said about Evan. The abuse wasn't as bad as I made it out to be."

The admission hung in the air like a lead weight, suffocating the room. Catherine's heart raced. She had suspected this, but hearing Vanessa say it out loud was something else entirely.

"You lied?" Catherine repeated, her voice low.

Vanessa wiped her eyes, her voice shaky. "I was angry. I wanted out of the marriage, and I knew that the only way to do it was to make Evan look like a monster. But you... you encouraged me. You made me believe that what I was feeling was abuse."

Catherine's chest tightened. The room felt like it was spinning. "I was trying to help you," she said defensively, though even to her own ears, her words sounded hollow.

"You pushed me, Catherine," Vanessa said, her voice rising. "You kept telling me that I was a victim, that Evan was dangerous. And I believed you because I wanted to believe it. I wanted to be the victim."

Catherine's mind reeled. She had always prided herself on helping women see the truth about their situations, helping them escape the abuse they couldn't recognize on their own. But had she pushed too hard? Had she projected her own trauma onto Vanessa, forcing her to see abuse where there was none?

Vanessa stood, her hands shaking. "I'm going to the media tomorrow. I'm going to tell them everything. I can't keep lying anymore."

"No," Catherine said quickly, standing up to face her. "Vanessa, if you do that, it will destroy both of us. Don't you see? We've come too far."

Vanessa shook her head, backing away. "I can't live with this anymore, Catherine. I'm sorry."

Before Catherine could say another word, Vanessa turned and left, the sound of the door closing echoing through the now eerily silent house.

The following morning, the headlines exploded. Vanessa had gone public with her confession, and the fallout was immediate. Catherine's phone rang incessantly—calls from journalists, former clients, and her attorney. Her reputation was in freefall.

By midday, Catherine sat in Daniel's office, the tension between them thick as smoke.

"We're in serious trouble," Daniel said, pacing the room. "Vanessa's public confession has opened the floodgates. More of your former clients are coming forward, claiming you manipulated them, too."

Catherine stared blankly ahead, her mind unable to process the words. Everything she had built, every client she had helped, was unraveling before her eyes. And now, she had to face the terrifying reality that perhaps she wasn't the hero she had always believed herself to be.

Chapter 7: A Dark Revelation

The evening light filtered through the large windows of Catherine's office, casting long shadows across the minimalist decor. The walls, usually a comforting sanctuary of muted tones and framed certificates, seemed to close in on her. Catherine sat behind her desk, tapping her pen lightly against her notepad, her mind racing. She knew this meeting was coming—Vanessa had been increasingly elusive, her responses vague, her tone less deferential. Something was off, and Catherine could feel the tremor beneath the surface of their once-perfect alliance.

A sharp knock interrupted her thoughts. Vanessa entered, her heels clicking on the polished floor, her face framed by a tension that Catherine hadn't seen before. She looked different, less vulnerable, more assured. Catherine's instincts prickled; this was not the Vanessa she had guided, the woman who had poured her soul out in this very office, detailing a husband's cruel emotional manipulation. No, this Vanessa was a threat.

"Vanessa," Catherine greeted, trying to keep her voice steady, warm. "I wasn't expecting you today."

"I think we need to talk," Vanessa said bluntly, ignoring the pleasantries, as she sat across from Catherine, her gaze unwavering.

The room seemed colder now. Catherine shifted in her chair, watching Vanessa carefully. Something was coming—something that could shatter everything.

"Talk?" Catherine echoed. "Of course. What's on your mind?"

Vanessa's lips tightened into a thin line. She was silent for a moment, her eyes darting toward the window as if deciding how to begin. When she finally spoke, her words were like a blade, slicing through the calm Catherine had tried to maintain.

"I need to come clean, Catherine. About everything."

The air between them thickened. Catherine felt her heartbeat quicken, but she kept her expression neutral. She had dealt with confessions before, with clients backtracking, feeling the weight of their decisions. But something about Vanessa's tone was different—it was too composed, too rehearsed.

"I'm not sure what you mean," Catherine said, her voice carefully measured, though her pulse pounded in her ears.

Vanessa leaned forward, her fingers tapping lightly against her purse, a gesture Catherine recognized from their sessions—nervous energy, anticipation.

"I exaggerated, Catherine. A lot. And I think... I think you knew it." Vanessa's eyes locked onto Catherine's, challenging her to deny it.

Catherine's breath caught in her throat. She had expected doubts, maybe even guilt. But an admission like this? Out loud? In her office?

"I'm not sure where this is coming from, Vanessa. We worked together, and—"

"No," Vanessa cut in, her voice sharp. "I mean, yes, we did. But you pushed me, Catherine. You wanted me to say more, to believe that my situation was worse than it was. And I let you because it felt good. You made me feel like I was a victim, like I was brave for standing up to Evan. But the truth is..." Vanessa hesitated, her eyes narrowing, "...I just wanted out of my marriage."

Catherine felt a chill crawl up her spine. Her mind raced, searching for the right response, something to control the spiraling conversation. But Vanessa wasn't done.

"I played along because you made it so easy. You gave me the narrative, the support, the way out. And now, I'm supposed to live with the consequences of that lie. I'm not sure I can anymore."

For a moment, the room was silent, the weight of Vanessa's words sinking in. Catherine's mind whirled. Her reputation, her career, her very identity, rested on Vanessa's story being true—or at least believable. This couldn't be happening. Not now.

"I never forced you into anything," Catherine said, her voice tight, controlled. "I guided you based on what you told me. You were the one who described the abuse, who came to me looking for help."

Vanessa shook her head, her expression turning hard. "You didn't force me, no. But you shaped it. Every time I hesitated, every time I said something that didn't quite fit your narrative, you nudged me, you filled in the gaps. You told me I was a victim, and after a while, I started to believe it."

Catherine leaned back in her chair, trying to keep her composure. She had heard this before—clients twisting things when they felt regret, trying to rewrite their own histories. It was common, especially in cases like this. But Vanessa... Vanessa was dangerous. Too much was at stake.

"You can't pin this on me," Catherine said, her voice firm, though there was a tremor of panic beneath it. "You knew what you were doing, Vanessa. You wanted to win, to get out of that marriage, to make a statement. And I helped you. I gave you the tools, but you chose to use them."

Vanessa's expression shifted, a flicker of something dark passing over her features. "Maybe I did. But now? Now, I'm going to tell the truth. The real truth."

Catherine felt the floor drop out from under her. This was it. The moment she had feared since the whispers first started, since those first clients had hinted that maybe, just maybe, they hadn't been as victimized as they'd thought. And now, Vanessa—her star client, the case that had solidified her reputation—was threatening to tear it all down.

"You're not thinking clearly," Catherine said, her voice low, almost pleading. "If you go public with this, you'll destroy everything. Your life, your reputation—do you really want to be known as the woman who cried wolf?"

Vanessa stood up, her eyes cold, distant. "I think I'd rather be known as the woman who told the truth, Catherine. Whatever the cost."

Catherine's mind raced, her thoughts a blur of panic and desperation. She had to stop this, had to control the narrative, had to make Vanessa see reason. But the woman standing before her was no longer the vulnerable socialite desperate for an escape. This Vanessa was a threat—a threat to everything Catherine had built.

As Vanessa turned to leave, Catherine's voice broke through the silence, sharp and commanding.

"If you do this, Vanessa, I will destroy you. You think you can just walk away from this, from everything we've built? Think again."

Vanessa paused, her hand on the doorknob. She turned slowly, her expression unreadable.

"You already did, Catherine. You just don't realize it yet."

And with that, she was gone, leaving Catherine standing alone in the fading light, the weight of her impending downfall pressing down on her like a vice.

The door clicked shut, and Catherine stood motionless, her mind still reeling from the confrontation. Vanessa's words echoed in her head, each syllable a nail driven into the carefully constructed façade she had built over the years. She had always prided herself on her ability to control situations, to guide her clients to the truth—even if that truth sometimes needed a little... embellishment. But this? This was different.

For the first time in years, Catherine felt fear. Real, bone-deep fear. If Vanessa went public, if she told the world that her story had been manipulated, Catherine's career would be over. The media, the legal system, her clients—everyone would turn on her. And the worst part was, she couldn't completely deny what Vanessa had said. Because, in her heart, Catherine knew that she had crossed lines. Lines she had sworn never to cross.

She walked slowly to the window, staring out at the city below. The sun was setting, casting a reddish hue over the skyline, a reminder that darkness was fast approaching. And for the first time in a long time, Catherine wasn't sure she could stop it.

She had always been the one with the power, the one in control. But now? Now, the tables were turning. And Catherine Faber, the celebrated psychologist, the hero to countless women, was about to face a reckoning.

The question was, how far was she willing to go to stop it?

Catherine sat in her office, the air thick with the weight of Vanessa's confession, still echoing in her mind. Vanessa's words had sliced through her carefully constructed world, leaving a jagged wound. She knows. Catherine could still feel the cold shock coursing through her, her hands trembling slightly as she clutched her phone. She had been so certain—so convinced of her role as savior. But now, the certainty had begun to crumble, and all that was left was the dizzying swirl of doubt.

She stared at the screen in front of her. Headlines from various news outlets blinked back at her, flashing in bold letters that seemed to grow larger with every second. Her name was still untarnished, but the storm was brewing. If Vanessa followed through on her threat, everything Catherine had worked for would be destroyed in an instant.

Her finger hovered over the phone, contemplating calling Vanessa again. She wanted to plead, to reason, to threaten—but she knew it wouldn't help. Vanessa had power now, and she knew how to wield it.

How had she let it come to this?

The silence of her office was deafening. Even the rhythmic ticking of the clock felt accusatory, marking the seconds that ticked away from her last semblance of control. Catherine's mind raced as she considered her options, though each potential path seemed darker and more dangerous than the last.

She couldn't shake the feeling that this was no longer about Vanessa. Vanessa was a symptom of something much larger—Catherine's own failings. She knew she had pushed too far, crossed too many ethical boundaries. She had wanted to help, of course, but in the pursuit of that help, she had projected her own pain onto the women who sought her guidance. She had shaped their narratives, made their trauma fit her own, and now it was all unraveling.

What had she done?

Her breath quickened as she rose from her desk, pacing the length of the room. She couldn't afford to lose control. Not now. Not when everything she had built—her career, her reputation, her legacy—was at stake. She needed to think, needed to act.

Catherine reached for the bottle of scotch in the corner of her office, pouring a glass with shaking hands. The amber liquid swirled in the glass, the scent both comforting and foreboding. She took a sip, feeling the burn as it slid down her throat, momentarily dulling the panic gnawing at her insides.

There had to be a way out of this.

She pulled up Vanessa's number on her phone again, her thumb hovering over the call button. But what could she say? The last conversation had left her shaken to her core. Vanessa had been calm, almost chilling in her confidence. The woman Catherine had thought she was saving had revealed herself to be far more dangerous than Catherine could have ever anticipated.

Vanessa had spun her web perfectly, and now, Catherine was trapped.

She slammed the phone down on the desk, her frustration bubbling over. This wasn't how it was supposed to go. She had been the savior, the advocate, the one who rescued women from the men who sought to destroy them. But now, the roles had been reversed. Vanessa had turned the tables, and Catherine was the one teetering on the edge of destruction.

Catherine's mind raced with possible solutions. She considered calling her lawyer, but the thought of involving more people made her stomach churn. If this got out, it would be the end of her career. No one would believe that her intentions had been pure, not once Vanessa's story hit the headlines.

There has to be another way, she thought, her pulse quickening.

She sat down again, opening her laptop. With a few quick keystrokes, she began researching damage control strategies. Her publicist had always warned her about the importance of maintaining control over the narrative, and now that advice seemed more critical than ever.

Her fingers drummed nervously on the desk as she skimmed articles on crisis management, but nothing seemed to fit her situation. This wasn't just a scandal she could spin or a story she could shape. This was her life's work, her entire identity, about to be shattered.

Her thoughts were interrupted by a knock on the door. She stiffened, her mind immediately jumping to the worst-case scenario. Had Vanessa already gone to the press? Was this the beginning of the end?

"Come in," she called, her voice betraying none of the panic that swirled within her.

Her assistant, Laura, stepped into the room, her expression hesitant. "I... I just wanted to check if everything's okay," she said softly. "You seemed... off earlier."

Catherine forced a smile, though she knew it didn't reach her eyes. "I'm fine. Just... a lot on my mind."

Laura nodded, but the concern in her eyes remained. She lingered for a moment longer before offering a tentative smile. "If you need anything, just let me know."

"I will," Catherine replied, her voice tight. "Thank you, Laura."

As the door closed behind her, Catherine exhaled shakily. She couldn't afford to lose her composure in front of her staff. They looked up to her, admired her. If they sensed any weakness, any crack in her façade, it would only accelerate her downfall.

Keep it together. You've faced worse. You can handle this.

But even as she tried to convince herself, the doubt crept in. She had never faced anything like this before. This wasn't just about saving her reputation—it was about saving herself from the truth she had been running from for years.

The scotch wasn't enough to steady her anymore. She needed a plan. Fast.

Her mind flickered back to the files she kept locked away. The ones with the details of her clients' cases. She had been meticulous in her documentation, always careful to keep records that could protect her if anything went wrong. But now, as she thought about those files, she felt a wave of nausea.

What if they dig too deep?

She stood up suddenly, walking to the filing cabinet in the corner of the room. Her hands trembled as she unlocked it, pulling out the thick folder labeled Vanessa Hale. She hesitated for a moment, her heart pounding in her chest, before flipping it open.

Inside were notes from their sessions, emails, text messages—everything that documented their interactions from the beginning. As she scanned through the pages, a sinking feeling settled in the pit of her stomach. There were too many moments where she had crossed the line, too many instances where she had pushed Vanessa to see herself as a victim.

I didn't mean to manipulate her, Catherine told herself. I was just trying to help.

But even as she tried to justify her actions, she couldn't shake the feeling that she had lost her way somewhere along the line. She had let her own trauma cloud her judgment, had let her need to save others blind her to the damage she was causing.

And now, it was all coming back to haunt her.

She closed the folder with a snap, her hands shaking as she returned it to the drawer. She couldn't let anyone see this. Not yet. Not until she figured out how to spin the story in her favor.

Her phone buzzed on the desk, and she glanced at the screen, her heart skipping a beat when she saw Vanessa's name. She hesitated for a moment before picking it up.

"Catherine," Vanessa's voice was cool, detached. "I've thought about our conversation. I'm willing to give you some time. But you know what I want."

Catherine swallowed hard, her throat dry. "Vanessa, please. We can work this out. You don't have to do this."

There was a pause on the other end of the line, and for a moment, Catherine dared to hope that Vanessa would change her mind. But when she spoke again, her voice was as cold as ever.

"You know what I need, Catherine. And if you don't give it to me, I'll go public. You won't just lose your career—you'll lose everything."

The line went dead, leaving Catherine in a suffocating silence. Her hands clenched into fists as she stared at the phone, the weight of Vanessa's threat pressing down on her chest.

Everything was falling apart. And it was all her fault.

She had spent years building her life around the idea that she was a hero, a savior of women in need. But now, as the walls closed in around her, Catherine realized that she had been lying to herself all along.

She wasn't the savior. She was the villain.

And there was no one left to save her.

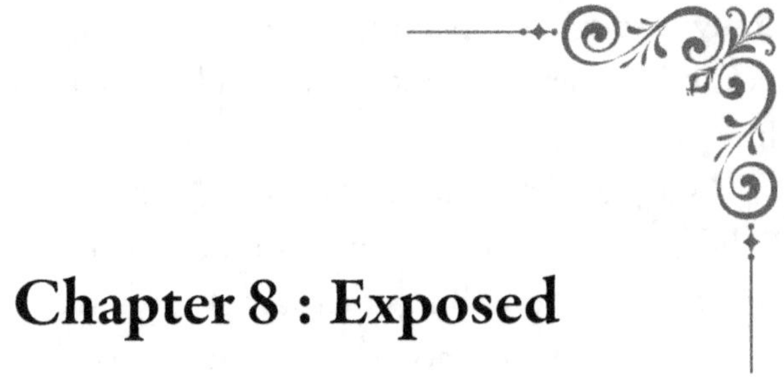

Chapter 8 : Exposed

Catherine Faber sat in her office, the sunlight pouring through the wide windows, illuminating the sleek, modern furniture that once exuded power and success. Now, it felt hollow—an illusion of control slipping from her grasp. She stared at her phone, her hand trembling slightly as she scrolled through the latest headlines. Every news outlet had latched onto the story, each one more vicious than the last.

"Psychologist Manipulates Clients into False Memories—Famed Advocate Under Fire"

"Catherine Faber: Hero or Villain? Former Clients Speak Out"

The words blurred together, but their weight crushed her. The media had turned on her with a speed that left her breathless. For years, she had been the darling of the public, a savior to countless women trapped in abusive relationships. But now, they were stripping her reputation away piece by piece, and Catherine was powerless to stop it.

The lawsuit had been filed by one of her former clients, a woman named Emily Reid. Emily had come to Catherine years ago, fragile and broken, convinced that her marriage was suffocating her. Catherine had seen the signs of abuse—gaslighting, manipulation, control. She had guided

Emily through the painful process of leaving her husband, of reclaiming her life. But now, Emily was saying something different.

"She planted the idea in my head," Emily had told the press. "I didn't think I was a victim until she convinced me that I was. I started to believe things that weren't even true."

It was the first accusation, but it wouldn't be the last. Within hours, other former clients had begun to come forward, each one echoing Emily's claims. They described how Catherine had subtly steered them toward narratives of abuse, how she had made them question their own memories, their own realities. They were accusing her of malpractice—of psychological manipulation.

Catherine felt her stomach twist in knots as the magnitude of the situation hit her. Everything she had built was collapsing around her, and there was no escape. Her entire career, her entire life, was being dismantled in front of her eyes. She had spent decades helping women escape their abusers, but now she was the one being accused of abuse. The irony was sickening.

The phone rang, snapping her out of her daze. It was her lawyer, Greg Thorne. She hesitated before answering, knowing that whatever he had to say would only make things worse.

"Catherine," Greg's voice was tense. "We need to talk about the lawsuit. Emily's testimony is gaining traction, and more women are coming forward. The media's all over this."

"I know," Catherine whispered. "I've seen the headlines."

"This isn't just about your reputation anymore. It's about legal ramifications. If enough clients come forward, you could be facing multiple malpractice suits. You could lose your license, Catherine."

Lose her license. The words hit her like a punch to the gut. She had worked her entire life to become who she was. Her career was everything—without it, she was nothing.

"I didn't do what they're accusing me of," she said, her voice shaking. "I helped them. They were victims, Greg. I just... I just helped them see the truth."

"I believe you," Greg said carefully. "But the problem is, they're saying you manipulated them into believing things that weren't true. The court is going to look at the evidence, and right now, public opinion is already against you."

Catherine closed her eyes, trying to hold back the tears threatening to spill. She couldn't afford to break down now. Not when everything was on the line.

"Is there anything we can do?" she asked, her voice barely audible.

"We need to fight this in court. We'll gather evidence, counter their claims, but Catherine... we need to be realistic about what we're up against. The media is turning this into a public trial. Even if we win in court, your reputation might not survive this."

She didn't respond. The truth was, she already knew that. The whispers had started long before Emily Reid went public. Former clients had been expressing doubts for months, quietly questioning the memories Catherine had helped them recover, the conclusions she had guided them toward. But she had never thought it would escalate to this.

"I'll be in touch soon," Greg said before hanging up.

Catherine placed the phone down and stared at her hands, feeling a strange sense of detachment from her own body. Her mind raced back to Vanessa Hale, the woman whose case had brought her into the spotlight, the woman who had made her a household name. Vanessa had accused her husband, Evan Hale, of horrific abuse—both physical and psychological. Catherine had believed every word, and with her guidance, Vanessa had torn him apart in court.

But what if Vanessa's story hadn't been entirely true?

The thought was unbearable, but it had been creeping into her mind for weeks. Vanessa had hinted that she might have exaggerated some details, that perhaps things weren't as clear-cut as she'd originally claimed. And Catherine... Catherine had ignored the warning signs. She had pushed Vanessa to tell her story, to shape it into something that aligned with Catherine's own understanding of abuse. Because to Catherine, all men like Evan Hale were abusers. They had to be.

The knock on the door startled her. Catherine stood up, quickly composing herself before opening it. Her assistant, Karen, stood on the other side, looking hesitant.

"Dr. Faber," Karen began cautiously, "there's someone here to see you."

"I'm not taking any appointments today," Catherine replied, her voice firmer than she felt.

"I know, but... it's Emily Reid. She's here. She says she wants to talk."

The blood drained from Catherine's face. Emily? Here? After everything?

"She's waiting in the lobby," Karen added, glancing nervously toward the hallway. "Should I tell her to leave?"

Catherine hesitated, her mind racing. The last thing she wanted was a confrontation, but maybe... maybe this was her chance to fix things. To explain, to make Emily understand that she had never meant to harm her.

"No," Catherine said finally. "I'll see her."

Karen nodded and disappeared down the hall, leaving Catherine to gather her thoughts. She took a deep breath, trying to steady the nerves swirling in her stomach, before walking out of her office and down the long, quiet corridor to the lobby.

Emily was standing by the window, looking out at the bustling city below. She turned when she heard Catherine's footsteps, her expression guarded. The woman who had once been fragile and unsure now stood tall, her demeanor cold and distant.

"Emily," Catherine greeted her, forcing a smile. "It's... it's good to see you."

"I'm sure it is," Emily replied, her voice flat. "Can we talk somewhere private?"

Catherine nodded and led her to one of the smaller conference rooms, where they could speak without being overheard. She closed the door behind them and gestured for Emily to sit, but Emily remained standing, her arms crossed.

"I didn't expect to see you here," Catherine began cautiously. "I know things have been... difficult."

"Difficult?" Emily's eyes flashed with anger. "You ruined my life, Catherine. You convinced me I was a victim, that my husband was abusing me when he wasn't. You made me believe things that weren't true, and now... now I can't even trust my own memories."

Catherine flinched at the accusation, but she forced herself to stay calm. She had to control the narrative.

"I never intended to hurt you, Emily. I thought... I thought I was helping you."

"No," Emily shot back, her voice rising. "You were helping yourself. You projected your own trauma onto me—onto all of us. You saw abuse where there wasn't any because you needed to believe that all men were like your father. You manipulated me, Catherine. You made me doubt myself, and now I can't even trust my own mind."

The words cut deep, but Catherine couldn't let them sink in. She couldn't let Emily's version of the story be the final word.

"I was trying to protect you," she insisted. "I saw the signs of abuse, and I... I just wanted to make sure you were safe."

"Safe?" Emily laughed bitterly. "Do I look safe to you? My marriage is over. My husband left me because of you. My life is a mess because of you."

Catherine's heart pounded in her chest. She had always believed she was doing the right thing, but now... now it felt like the ground was shifting beneath her feet. What if she had been wrong?

"I didn't mean for any of this to happen," Catherine said quietly. "I'm sorry, Emily. I'm truly sorry."

But the apology did little to soften the anger in Emily's eyes.

"It's too late for that," Emily replied coldly. "You're going to pay for what you did, Catherine. I'll make sure of it."

With those final words, Emily turned and walked out, leaving Catherine alone in the room. The door clicked shut, and for the first time, Catherine felt the full weight of what she had done. The walls seemed to close in on her, the air growing thick with guilt and fear.

Her entire career had been built on the belief that she was helping women escape abuse, that she was fighting against the very thing that had destroyed her own family. But now... now she had to face the possibility that she had become the very thing she despised.

As the minutes ticked by, Catherine remained frozen in the empty room, her mind racing with questions she didn't have the answers to. The world outside continued on without her, but inside, everything had come to a standstill.

Because for the first time, Catherine Faber wasn't sure if she was the hero of her story—or the villain.

The courthouse was swarming with people. Journalists jockeyed for position, their camera lenses trained on the heavy wooden doors of the courtroom, where Catherine Faber's fate would soon be decided. The morning sun cast long shadows over the crowd, but the air was thick with anticipation and tension. Catherine, for the first time in her career, was not here as an expert witness or a beacon of hope for the wronged. She was the accused, and the world was watching.

Inside the courtroom, the atmosphere was no less intense. Rows of spectators, reporters, and legal teams filled the gallery, their eyes fixed on the center stage where Catherine sat next to her defense attorney. Her once unshakeable confidence had eroded, her face a tight mask of restraint, but the cracks were visible. She shifted uncomfortably in her chair, her gaze wandering over the unfamiliar faces in the room—the judge, the jury, and the opposition counsel—all strangers who would soon pass judgment on her life's work.

The trial had become a media spectacle, a public dismantling of the woman once hailed as a champion of victims. For years, Catherine had guided others through the legal system, giving them the tools to break free from their abusers. Now, those same methods were under scrutiny, painted not as salvation but as manipulation.

The prosecution had laid out their case with brutal efficiency, parading former clients to the witness stand—each testimony a brick in the wall that was slowly closing in on Catherine. First, it was Karen Monroe, a name Catherine hadn't thought about in years. A woman whose tearful recounting of her "abusive" relationship had once been a small but significant victory for Catherine's growing career. Now, Karen sat on the witness stand, her voice steady, her demeanor composed, as she recounted a very different version of her experience.

"I came to Dr. Faber for help," Karen began, glancing at Catherine with a mixture of disappointment and betrayal. "I was confused, unsure of what I was going through. My marriage wasn't perfect, but I didn't think of myself as a victim—not at first."

The prosecutor, a lean man with sharp features, nodded sympathetically, allowing Karen the space to continue. "What changed?" he asked.

"Dr. Faber... she helped me see things differently. She told me that emotional abuse can be subtle, that it can look like normal behavior if you don't know what to look for. At first, I was grateful. But over time, I started to doubt my own memories. She encouraged me to focus on the negative parts of my relationship, and the more we talked, the more I began to believe I was being manipulated by my husband."

"Did you believe that at the time?" the prosecutor pressed.

Karen hesitated. "I thought I did. But looking back... I'm not sure anymore. I don't know if I was really a victim or if I was led to believe I was."

It was a damning statement, one that landed with a heavy silence in the courtroom. Catherine's lawyer rose to cross-examine, attempting to cast doubt on Karen's new perspective, but the damage was done. The seed of doubt had been planted, and Catherine could feel the weight of it pressing down on her.

More witnesses followed. Women who had once praised Catherine for her guidance now sat in judgment of her. Some cried as they spoke, others remained coldly detached, but the story was always the same. Catherine had pushed them, shaped their narratives, and in some cases, convinced them that they had suffered abuse where there might have been none.

As the testimonies mounted, the prosecution's case became clear: Catherine Faber wasn't just a psychologist helping women reclaim their lives—she was a puppeteer, pulling the strings to mold her clients' experiences into something that fit her own narrative. The line between advocate and abuser had blurred, and Catherine now found herself on the wrong side of it.

By midday, the prosecution rested. Catherine's lawyer, Steven Holloway, stood and adjusted his tie. He was a seasoned litigator, sharp and deliberate, but even he seemed weary from the relentless assault on Catherine's character. The defense had to walk a fine line—discrediting the testimonies of former clients without appearing to attack victims. It was a nearly impossible task.

As Holloway approached the jury, his voice took on a calm, reasoned tone. "Ladies and gentlemen of the jury, what we've heard today are deeply personal and emotional stories. I don't dispute that these women had difficult experiences. But we must ask ourselves: are these stories the result of abuse, or are they the result of misunderstood therapy?"

He turned to face the jury directly. "Dr. Faber dedicated her life to helping women who felt powerless, who had nowhere else to turn. She provided a safe space for them to process their emotions, to reflect on their relationships. Therapy is not an exact science. It's messy, it's complicated, and it's deeply subjective."

Holloway glanced back at Catherine, who sat rigid in her seat, her hands clasped tightly together. "Dr. Faber did not manipulate these women. She helped them see what they were unable to see on their own. And yes, in some cases, that meant confronting painful truths about their relationships. But that is not manipulation—that is therapy."

The argument was sound, logical even. But Catherine could see the skepticism in the jury's eyes. They weren't convinced. And why would they be? In a world obsessed with clear villains and heroes, her story was too murky, too complex. She was neither saint nor sinner—just a woman who had lost her way.

When the defense rested, the courtroom was still, the air heavy with anticipation. The judge called for a brief recess before closing arguments, and Catherine was escorted out of the courtroom by Holloway. As they moved through the halls, the sound of reporters shouting questions reached them through the walls.

"Catherine," Holloway said quietly, "you need to prepare yourself. This isn't looking good."

She didn't respond. What could she say? He was right, of course. The tide had turned against her, and there was little she could do to stop it.

After the recess, the courtroom filled once again. Catherine sat in her usual spot, her gaze unfocused as she listened to the final statements. The prosecutor's words were damning, painting Catherine as a woman consumed by her own trauma, desperate to control the lives of others to make sense of her own past. He spoke of power and responsibility, of how Catherine had abused both, leaving a trail of shattered lives in her wake.

When it was Holloway's turn, he did his best to salvage the situation. He spoke of Catherine's dedication, her good intentions, and the many lives she had genuinely helped. But it wasn't enough. The jury didn't want to hear about good intentions. They wanted a villain, and Catherine had been cast in that role.

As the jury filed out to deliberate, Catherine sat in silence, her mind racing. She had spent her entire life fighting against the very thing she had become. She had devoted herself to empowering women, to giving them the tools to escape manipulation, only to realize that she had been manipulating them all along.

Hours passed. The courtroom remained quiet, the tension building as everyone waited for the jury to return. Catherine's thoughts drifted back to her father—the man who had taught her everything she knew about control, about twisting the truth to fit his own narrative. She had spent so many years trying to escape his influence, but in the end, she had followed in his footsteps.

When the jury finally returned, the courtroom fell into a hush. The foreman rose, holding the verdict in his hands. Catherine's heart pounded in her chest, the sound of blood rushing in her ears as the judge called the court to order.

"On the charge of malpractice," the foreman began, his voice steady, "we find the defendant, Dr. Catherine Faber, guilty."

The words hit Catherine like a physical blow, knocking the air from her lungs. Guilty. It was over. Everything she had built, everything she had fought for, was gone. The judge's voice droned on, issuing the formalities of sentencing, but Catherine barely heard it. The weight of the verdict pressed down on her, suffocating her in its finality.

As she was led out of the courtroom in handcuffs, the flashes of cameras blinded her, and the shouts of reporters rang in her ears. Catherine Faber, once a celebrated psychologist and advocate, was now just another fallen figure in the public eye.

Chapter 9:
Unraveling the Lies

Catherine Faber stared at the news scrolling across her phone screen. Each headline that passed was another weight pressing down on her chest. "Former Clients Accuse Faber of Manipulation," "Catherine Faber's Methods Under Scrutiny," "Psychologist Turned Abuser?" The words seemed surreal, but they were her new reality. Just weeks ago, she had been celebrated as a hero, a savior for women escaping the clutches of abusive relationships. Now, she was vilified. The hero had become the villain.

She placed her phone face down on the kitchen counter, trying to ignore the tremble in her hands. She couldn't think straight anymore. Her once pristine world was crumbling, and it wasn't just because of the media—clients, former clients, were coming forward with damning stories. Stories that painted her as a manipulator, someone who twisted their trauma to fit a narrative she believed in more than they did. Was it true? Could she have done that?

Her mind flashed back to those sessions—those women, broken and confused, looking to her for guidance. She had felt so sure of her methods, so sure that she was doing the right thing. But as the accusations piled up, she couldn't shake the gnawing feeling that maybe, just maybe, she had pushed too hard. Maybe she had overstepped, projecting her pain onto them in ways she never realized.

The doorbell rang, breaking through the fog of her thoughts. Catherine hesitated, her heart pounding. Was it another reporter? Another lawyer? She moved toward the door, her bare feet padding softly on the hardwood floor. Through the peephole, she saw a familiar face—Karen, one of her oldest clients. For a moment, a flicker of hope bloomed in Catherine's chest. Karen had always been one of her greatest successes, a woman who had left an abusive marriage and rebuilt her life. Surely, Karen had come to offer support.

Catherine opened the door, a weak smile on her face. "Karen, I—"

Karen didn't return the smile. Instead, her lips were set in a thin, tight line, her eyes hard. "I need to talk to you," she said, her voice cold.

Catherine stepped aside, letting Karen enter the house. The two women stood awkwardly in the living room, the air thick with unspoken tension.

"Can I get you something? Tea, coffee?" Catherine offered, hoping to diffuse the palpable tension.

"No, Catherine," Karen said, her voice cutting. "I'm not here for small talk."

Catherine swallowed, her heart sinking. "What's going on?"

Karen crossed her arms, her gaze fixed on Catherine. "You know what's going on. Everyone's talking. You've seen the news. Former clients—women like me—are coming forward, saying that you manipulated them, that you convinced them they were victims when they weren't."

"That's not true," Catherine protested weakly. "I helped those women. I helped you."

Karen's eyes flared with something akin to anger. "Did you help me, Catherine? Or did you just make me see things the way you wanted me to? I've been thinking a lot about those sessions we had—about the things you said, the questions you asked. You made me doubt my own memories, made me think that everything was worse than it actually was."

"That's not true," Catherine whispered, her throat tightening. But as she spoke, doubt crept into her voice. Had she done that?

Karen's face softened slightly, but her tone remained firm. "I know you've been through hell, Catherine. I know what your father did to you, and I'm not here to hurt you. But I can't ignore the fact that you pushed me—pushed all of us—into believing that our situations were worse than they were."

Catherine's legs felt weak, and she sank into the nearest chair. "I only wanted to help," she murmured, more to herself than to Karen.

"Maybe you did," Karen said, her voice gentler now. "But you crossed a line. You projected your pain onto me, onto others. You twisted our stories into something they weren't."

Catherine looked up, tears pricking at the corners of her eyes. "Karen, I—I didn't mean to. I swear, I thought I was doing the right thing."

"I believe you," Karen said softly. "But that doesn't change the fact that you hurt people. You've been so blinded by your own trauma that you couldn't see the damage you were causing."

The weight of Karen's words pressed down on Catherine like a physical force. All her life, she had believed that she was fighting against abusers, protecting the vulnerable. But now, she couldn't help but wonder if she had become the very thing she despised.

After Karen left, Catherine sat in silence, staring at the wall. She could hear the ticking of the clock on the mantel, the sound unnervingly loud in the quiet house. Every tick seemed to echo inside her head, each second bringing with it a new wave of doubt and guilt.

Her phone buzzed on the counter, but she ignored it. She knew what it was—more emails, more notifications, more people distancing themselves from her. She had become toxic. Even her closest friends were staying away, not wanting to be associated with the scandal that was enveloping her life.

Catherine stood up, pacing the room. She needed to clear her head, to think. She couldn't just let everything fall apart. She was Catherine Faber, a woman who had built an empire on helping others. She couldn't let a few accusations destroy her career, her reputation. There had to be a way to salvage this.

Her thoughts turned to Vanessa Hale. It all started with her. Vanessa had been the catalyst for this disaster. She was the one who had lied, the one who had exaggerated her story for attention and fame. Catherine had only tried to help, to guide her through the process. She had never intended for things to spiral out of control like this.

Vanessa. That name echoed in her mind like a bitter taste on her tongue. Vanessa had used her, twisted her guidance into a weapon to destroy Evan Hale. And now, Catherine was the one paying the price.

She grabbed her phone and scrolled through her contacts until she found Vanessa's name. Her finger hovered over the call button. She needed answers. She needed to confront Vanessa, to make her understand the damage she had caused.

But as her finger hovered over the screen, a sudden realization hit her. Vanessa wasn't the only one responsible. Catherine had played a part in this too. She had pushed Vanessa, just as Karen had said. She had seen Vanessa's story through the lens of her own trauma and had guided her down a path that may not have been entirely true.

With a shaking hand, Catherine put the phone down. The weight of her actions settled over her like a heavy fog. She couldn't deny it any longer—she had crossed a line. Maybe not intentionally, but she had. And now, she had to face the consequences.

The next morning, Catherine woke to the sound of her phone ringing. Groggy and disoriented, she fumbled for it on the bedside table. The name on the screen made her heart skip a beat—Evan Hale's lawyer.

For a moment, she considered ignoring the call. But she knew that would only make things worse. Taking a deep breath, she answered.

"Ms. Faber," the lawyer's voice was cool and professional. "I'm calling to inform you that we will be moving forward with the defamation lawsuit. We believe we have sufficient evidence to prove that you coerced Vanessa Hale into fabricating her allegations against my client."

Catherine's stomach twisted. "That's not true," she stammered. "I never coerced anyone."

The lawyer was silent for a moment, then sighed. "Ms. Faber, I suggest you speak with your attorney. This situation is only going to escalate from here."

The call ended, leaving Catherine in stunned silence. She stared at the phone, her mind racing. A lawsuit? She had never imagined it would come to this. But now, it seemed inevitable.

Catherine stood up, her body moving on autopilot as she walked to the window. She looked out at the world beyond, feeling more isolated than ever. She had spent her life fighting for justice, for truth, for victims of abuse. But now, she was the one being accused.

Her reflection stared back at her from the glass, and for the first time in her life, Catherine didn't recognize the woman looking back at her.

The weeks that followed were a blur of legal battles and media scrutiny. Former clients continued to come forward, each one adding another layer to the mounting accusations against Catherine. Her reputation was in tatters, and her once-pristine career was on the verge of complete collapse.

The final blow came when Vanessa Hale gave an exclusive interview, painting herself as a victim of Catherine's coercion. "I trusted her," Vanessa had said, her voice filled with emotion. "But she pushed me to say things, to believe things that weren't true. She made me feel like I had to be a victim, even when I wasn't."

As Catherine watched the interview from the solitude of her living room, she felt something inside her break. Vanessa had distanced herself from the scandal, leaving Catherine to bear the brunt of the fallout. The woman who had once been her greatest success had now become her greatest undoing.

Catherine Faber had built her life on helping others escape their abusers. But now, as her world crumbled around her, she couldn't escape the truth—she had become the abuser in her own story.

Vanessa Hale sat across from the television, her eyes fixated on the screen. Every channel was now consumed with the scandal, a rapid descent that once seemed impossible for the untouchable Catherine Faber. The headline banner at the bottom of the screen read, "Psychologist Catherine Faber Faces Malpractice Allegations—Former Clients Speak Out." Vanessa smiled faintly, the corners of her lips curling in satisfaction. She had pulled it off—she had escaped unscathed while Catherine's world crumbled.

Catherine had been her savior once. At least, that's what Vanessa told herself in the beginning. She had gone to Catherine desperate, exhausted from the life she lived with Evan. Sure, things hadn't been perfect in her marriage, but abusive? She hadn't considered the word until Catherine introduced it, dangling the possibility like bait. Slowly, over the months of therapy, Catherine had planted seeds in her mind, twisting memories of arguments and frustrations into something darker. It wasn't long before Vanessa began to adopt the narrative Catherine so desperately wanted her to believe.

But now, Vanessa felt a sick thrill. She had taken Catherine's manipulation and turned it on its head, using it to her own advantage. Catherine had wanted a victim, but Vanessa had seen an opportunity for freedom and fame. Her escape plan had worked, and now, as Catherine's reputation disintegrated, Vanessa found herself in a position she had always coveted: the center of attention, but now as a survivor rather than a victim.

The media storm had shifted dramatically over the past few weeks. As more of Catherine's former clients came forward, the narrative surrounding the high-profile psychologist shifted from hero to villain. Vanessa, ever the actress, knew how to play her part well. In carefully crafted interviews, she cast herself as yet another casualty of Catherine's coercion. She was no longer the poor, abused wife trying to escape her cruel husband—she was a victim of Catherine's manipulative methods.

Vanessa stood and walked over to the window, the city sprawling beneath her feet. Her phone buzzed on the kitchen counter, the screen lighting up with a call from her publicist. She ignored it. For now, she had everything she wanted. She'd already made her next move.

Three Months Earlier

Vanessa watched as Catherine paced back and forth in her office, her brow furrowed in deep concentration. The court case against Evan had grown more complex than either of them had expected. Evan's legal team had been ruthless, digging into every detail of Vanessa's life, finding ways to poke holes in her story. The pressure weighed heavily on Catherine, and it was clear that she was starting to unravel.

"They're not going to stop," Catherine muttered under her breath. "They're going to keep coming after you, after me. We need to stay strong."

Vanessa leaned back in the leather chair, feigning concern. "But what if they find something? What if they don't believe me?"

"They have to believe you," Catherine insisted, her voice rising. "The truth is on our side. You are a victim, Vanessa, and they can't deny that."

Vanessa held back a smirk. The truth? She had started to wonder if Catherine even knew what the truth was anymore. The lines between reality and fiction had blurred months ago, ever since Catherine began pushing her to remember things differently. Every session with her therapist became another exercise in reshaping her past—turning arguments into abuse, disappointment into cruelty.

It wasn't that Evan had been perfect. He had his flaws, certainly. But the monster Catherine had helped her create? That was something else entirely. And now Vanessa was beginning to see a way out, one where she could leave her marriage, secure her freedom, and even gain public sympathy in the process.

Present Day

Vanessa's carefully constructed plan had been in motion for months. The moment Catherine suggested taking her story public, Vanessa had known how she would turn the tables. The lawsuit against Evan had gone better than expected, with Vanessa walking away as a sympathetic figure. But as doubts began to arise about the authenticity of her story, she needed a scapegoat—and Catherine had provided herself on a silver platter.

She had distanced herself from Catherine just as the first signs of trouble began to surface. Publicly, she expressed gratitude for Catherine's help but began hinting at the pressures she felt during therapy. In interviews, Vanessa subtly implied that Catherine might have pushed her to exaggerate, painting herself as a victim once again—this time of Catherine's manipulations. The media ate it up.

Sitting down at the kitchen counter, Vanessa picked up her phone and opened her emails. A message from her publicist was at the top of her inbox, outlining the upcoming interviews she had scheduled. Vanessa had already signed a deal with a major network to tell her story—a tell-all interview that would further cement her place in the public eye.

In every appearance, Vanessa played her role perfectly. She was the wronged woman, the survivor, and now, the victim of a therapist gone too far. Her words were carefully chosen to deflect any blame from herself, and each time she hinted at Catherine's coercive tactics, the media latched on, tearing Catherine apart piece by piece.

Catherine, on the Other Side

Catherine Faber sat alone in her office, staring blankly at the stacks of papers scattered across her desk. Her career, once built on the promise of saving women, was now crumbling beneath her. The malpractice lawsuits were piling up, each one claiming the same thing—that she had manipulated vulnerable clients into believing they were victims of abuse.

Vanessa's betrayal had cut the deepest. Catherine had truly believed she was helping her, that Vanessa had been a genuine victim of an abusive marriage. But now, as the world turned against her, Catherine couldn't help but question everything. Had she pushed too hard? Had she, in her desperation to help, gone too far?

She opened her laptop, the harsh glow of the screen illuminating her face in the dim room. A news article popped up, the headline screaming: "Former Clients Accuse Famed

Psychologist of Coercion—How Catherine Faber Fell From Grace." Catherine scrolled through the article, her stomach churning with each word.

Vanessa had painted herself as the victim once again, this time at Catherine's expense. In an interview, she had claimed that Catherine pressured her into making the abuse sound worse than it was, suggesting that Catherine had a pattern of coercing her clients into believing they were more damaged than they truly were.

It was all lies.

Catherine knew the truth, or at least she thought she did. She had never coerced Vanessa, had never forced her to say anything she didn't believe. But the mounting evidence against her made it harder to hold on to that certainty. Had she crossed ethical boundaries without even realizing it?

The seeds of doubt had been planted, and now they were growing, threatening to swallow her whole.

Vanessa's Freedom

Vanessa was free, for the first time in years. She had played the game well—better than even she had anticipated. She had outsmarted Evan, outmaneuvered Catherine, and now stood in a position of power. The public loved her, the media painted her as a woman who had overcome not just one, but two manipulative figures in her life. She was a star, and the world was at her feet.

But deep down, Vanessa knew the truth. She had never been a victim. Not really. Evan hadn't been abusive—controlling, perhaps, but not the monster Catherine had convinced her he was. And Catherine? Catherine had been her enabler, her ticket out of a life she had grown tired of.

Now, as Vanessa prepared for her next chapter, she couldn't help but feel a twinge of guilt. Not for Evan, or even for Catherine, but for the person she had become in the process. The line between truth and lies had blurred so completely that even she had trouble keeping track of the real story. But in the end, it didn't matter. What mattered was that she had won.

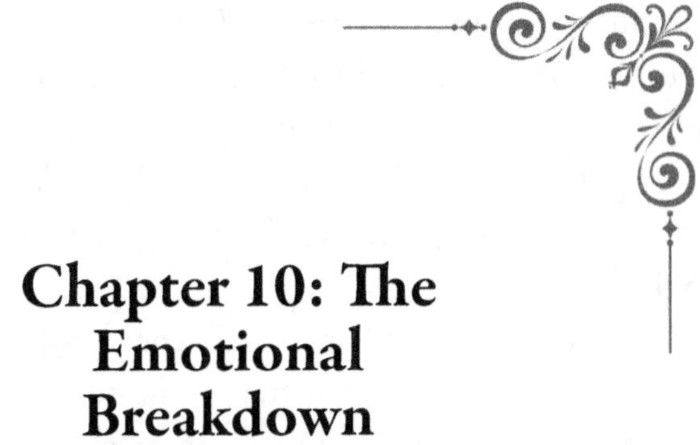

Chapter 10: The Emotional Breakdown

Catherine Faber sat in the corner of her darkened living room, staring blankly at the flickering television screen. The sound was on, but she wasn't listening. News anchors droned on about the latest scandal, rehashing the details of her spectacular fall from grace. Her name was once synonymous with empowerment and healing; now, it was linked with deception and malpractice. Her once pristine reputation had crumbled to dust in a matter of weeks, and she had nowhere to hide.

She blinked, feeling the familiar wave of nausea that always came with the memories she tried so hard to suppress. Her father's voice echoed in her mind, low and cruel, as it had been when she was a child. "You'll never be good enough. You're worthless. Can't you see that?" She squeezed her eyes shut, trying to block it out, but the memories pressed in on her, stronger now than ever.

For years, she'd buried the truth of her past, focusing all her energy on helping others—on rescuing women like her mother had once been. But in the end, it seemed that she had only been running from the inevitable. Her father's manipulative abuse had shaped her more than she ever wanted to admit. And now, in the wake of Vanessa Hale's public betrayal, Catherine had been forced to confront the truth: she wasn't just a victim of her father's cruelty. She had become a manipulator in her own right.

Her phone buzzed on the table next to her, but she ignored it. She already knew what the notifications would say—more journalists wanting a comment, more clients coming forward with accusations. Everyone wanted a piece of her, but there was nothing left to take. The irony of her situation wasn't lost on her. She had spent her entire career advocating for victims, only to find herself branded as an abuser in the court of public opinion.

She stood up, the weight of her exhaustion pressing down on her shoulders, and walked over to the window. Outside, the world continued to move, oblivious to her internal collapse. The streetlights cast long shadows across the empty road, and for a moment, she felt as though she was looking at a scene from her childhood—standing at the window of her childhood home, watching her father's car pull into the driveway, her stomach knotting in fear of what awaited inside.

Her mind was pulling her back there, to the root of it all. She could see her younger self, timid and desperate for approval, trying to stay invisible to avoid her father's wrath. And her mother, fragile and broken, who had done her best to protect Catherine from the worst of it but had been too weak to save herself.

Catherine pressed her forehead against the cool glass and breathed deeply, willing herself to stay present. But the flood of memories had begun, and there was no stopping them now.

The nightmares had started weeks ago, just after Vanessa's explosive confession to the media. In her dreams, Catherine was always a child again, cowering in the corner of the living room as her father's voice thundered over her. The fear was the same, but this time, she was aware of something else—a shadow of guilt lurking just behind the terror. It whispered to her in the dark, telling her that she had become like him, that she had hurt people the way he had hurt her.

It wasn't the first time she had considered the possibility. Over the years, she had brushed off the nagging doubts, telling herself that her methods were necessary. But now, with her life in ruins, she couldn't ignore the question any longer. Had she truly helped the women who had come to her for guidance? Or had she merely twisted their stories, making them fit the narrative she needed them to play out?

Sinking back into the armchair, Catherine hugged her knees to her chest, feeling more like a child than the seasoned professional she was supposed to be. The public had turned on her, but it wasn't just their judgment that weighed on her now. It was the weight of her own conscience, demanding answers she wasn't sure she could give.

The memories continued to surface over the following days, gnawing at her relentlessly. She tried to distract herself with work—drafting responses to her legal team, attempting to salvage what little was left of her practice—but nothing could keep the memories at bay for long. In the quiet moments, when she was alone in her apartment, they would come rushing back, leaving her breathless and shaken.

It wasn't just the memory of her father that haunted her. It was the realization that she had never truly healed from what he had done to her. Instead, she had channeled all her anger and pain into her work, using her clients' stories to relive her own trauma, over and over again. But instead of helping them escape their situations, she had pushed them further into victimhood, trapping them in the same cycle of fear and control that she had been trapped in as a child.

The full weight of her complicity was almost too much to bear. She had built her career on the promise of empowerment, but she had never truly believed in it—not for herself, and not for her clients. She had been playing a role, convincing herself that she was a savior, when in reality, she had been using her clients to fight a battle she could never win.

Her mind drifted back to Vanessa. The woman had been everything Catherine despised—privileged, shallow, and willing to do whatever it took to get what she wanted. But even now, Catherine couldn't entirely blame her. Vanessa had been desperate, just as Catherine had been once. Desperate to escape a life she felt trapped in, willing to grasp at any opportunity for freedom, even if it meant fabricating a story of abuse.

Catherine had seen the truth in Vanessa's eyes during their sessions. She had known, deep down, that Vanessa wasn't the victim she claimed to be. But instead of calling her out, Catherine had encouraged her to embellish her story, to make it more dramatic, more believable. She had been complicit in the lie because it had suited her purposes. Vanessa's case had been the perfect platform for Catherine to showcase her skills and reinforce her position as a leader in her field.

Now, that lie had come crashing down, and with it, everything Catherine had worked for.

The nights were the worst. Catherine found herself lying awake for hours, staring at the ceiling, her thoughts racing. She couldn't escape the feeling that her life had been a lie—everything she had achieved, everything she had believed in, all of it built on a foundation of manipulation and control. The truth of who she was, of what she had done, was more than she could handle.

Her father's voice echoed in her mind once more. "You'll never be good enough. You'll always be worthless." For so long, she had fought to prove him wrong, to show the world that she was strong and capable. But now, as she lay there in the dark, she wondered if he had been right all along.

The thought filled her with a sickening sense of dread. She had always prided herself on being in control, on having the power to change lives. But in the end, it seemed that she had been just as powerless as the women she had tried to help. Powerless to escape her past, powerless to change the trajectory of her own life.

By the time the sun rose each morning, Catherine was already exhausted, her body aching from the tension that had gripped her through the night. She moved through her days in a fog, barely registering the world around her. She stopped answering her phone, stopped responding to emails, stopped caring about the legal battles that loomed on the horizon. None of it seemed to matter anymore.

The only thing that occupied her mind now was the question she had been avoiding for so long: Had she become like her father? Had she, in her desperate attempt to save others, ended up perpetuating the same cycle of abuse that had destroyed her childhood?

The answer, when it finally came, was devastating. Yes. She had become like him. Not in the same overtly cruel way, but in the subtle, insidious way that only a person with deep, unresolved trauma could. She had manipulated her clients, twisting their stories to fit her own narrative, just as her father had twisted her sense of self-worth to suit his needs.

The realization hit her like a punch to the gut, leaving her gasping for air. She had spent her entire life fighting against the darkness her father had instilled in her, only to discover that it had been there all along, lurking just beneath the surface.

Catherine knew there was no going back now. The damage had been done—not just to her clients, but to herself. The person she had tried so hard to become was a lie, and the truth of who she really was would haunt her for the rest of her life.

The walls around Catherine Faber's life were crumbling faster than she could contain them. Her once-steady hands, that guided so many women toward salvation, now trembled uncontrollably as she stared at her reflection in the mirror. The woman looking back at her was a stranger—hollow eyes, thinning hair from the constant stress, and an expression that teetered between confusion and outright despair. The Catherine who had once stood tall, respected and revered, was gone, replaced by someone consumed by doubt and fear.

In her isolation, the memories became too much. The flashbacks of her father's cold, calculating voice took over. His words echoed in her mind: "You're nothing without me, Catherine. Everything you think you are—it's all because of me." The more she tried to suppress them, the more the memories flooded in, vivid and haunting. The man who had taken away her mother, had poisoned her childhood, now had complete control of her once again.

She had become the very thing she swore to fight against. She couldn't stop seeing it now, the parallels between her father's manipulations and her own subtle coercions with her clients. The realization that she had not saved Vanessa, nor any of her clients—she had molded them into her own perception of victimhood, driven by her unresolved need to fix the broken parts of her past—was unbearable.

Catherine had no appetite anymore, no desire to leave her house, no willingness to answer the incessant calls from the few friends who hadn't completely distanced themselves. She sat in silence for hours, her mind running through scenarios over and over, wondering how she let it all slip away.

The phone rang again, its shrill tone cutting through the stillness of her small, dark apartment. She ignored it, as she had for the past several days. She hadn't returned any calls, not from her colleagues, not from her legal team, not even from her mother's old friend, one of the few people who had truly known Catherine's past.

As the silence returned after the final ring, Catherine grabbed the bottle of red wine on the table beside her and poured herself another glass. Her hand shook as she brought it to her lips, spilling a few drops on her lap. It didn't matter. She couldn't remember the last time she had eaten, slept, or done anything that resembled living.

There was nothing left for her now. The lawsuits, the media frenzy—it was all closing in. Every headline, every news report tore into her like a fresh wound. "Catherine Faber: Hero or Villain?" "Psychologist's Empire Crumbles as Former Clients Speak Out." They had found more clients, more stories of coercion and manipulation. The faces of women she had once sat with in confidence, who had looked up to her as their savior, now stared back from the pages of tabloids and online blogs, condemning her. They weren't lying—she had crossed ethical lines. But Catherine had convinced herself, until now, that it was for their own good. She believed she was helping them.

Now, it was clear: she had only been helping herself.

The memories shifted again, this time back to her father's study. She was a child, barely eight years old, hiding behind the doorframe as her father berated her mother. His words were so precise, so cold, stripping her mother of her confidence, her sense of self. Catherine had watched, frozen in place, unable to save her. After her mother's death, that guilt became her constant companion. It followed her into her adult life, and it became the reason she vowed to never let another woman be victimized.

But she hadn't saved them. She had turned them into victims—just like her father had done to her mother.

A sharp knock at the door pulled her from her thoughts. She stood slowly, the room spinning slightly from the wine, and walked toward it. The person on the other side knocked again, more insistently this time.

"Catherine, open up. I know you're in there," the voice said, muffled by the door.

It was her colleague, Emma. They had worked together for years, but Catherine had avoided her for weeks now. She didn't want to face her, not with everything that was happening.

"Please, Catherine. You can't just hide away in here."

With a sigh, Catherine unlocked the door and pulled it open just enough for Emma to slip inside. She looked around the apartment—empty takeout containers, wine bottles, and scattered paperwork littered the room.

"Jesus, Catherine... You need help. This... this isn't you," Emma said, her voice filled with concern. She moved toward Catherine, but Catherine took a step back, retreating to her couch.

"I don't need help," Catherine muttered. "It's too late for that. Everything's falling apart, Emma. Everything."

Emma sat down across from her, looking at her with a mix of sympathy and frustration. "You can't give up like this. The lawsuits, the media—they'll pass. We can fight this."

But Catherine shook her head, tears finally brimming in her eyes. "I deserve it. Don't you get it? I deserve everything that's happening. I did this. I manipulated them. All of them. I pushed them into believing they were victims, just like I believed my mother was a victim. But maybe... maybe she wasn't. Maybe I've been wrong this whole time."

Emma blinked, stunned. "What are you saying?"

"I'm saying," Catherine's voice cracked, "that I don't know what's real anymore. I thought I was saving them, but I was just making them believe they were helpless. Just like my father made my mother believe she was helpless. I became him."

Emma stared at her, speechless for a moment. She had known Catherine for years, but she had never seen her like this—so defeated, so broken. "Catherine, you are not your father. You've helped so many women."

"No," Catherine interrupted, her voice suddenly sharp. "I've destroyed them. Don't you understand? I took their pain and twisted it, made it worse because I needed them to be victims. I needed them to be what I couldn't save my mother from being."

The room fell silent, the weight of Catherine's confession hanging in the air.

After Emma left, Catherine was once again alone, but the thoughts wouldn't stop. The memories wouldn't stop. Her clients' faces flashed in her mind—Vanessa, Maria, Jessica—so many women who had trusted her. And she had failed them all. She had let her past dictate their futures.

She picked up her phone, her fingers trembling as she scrolled through the messages. Lawsuits, press inquiries, emails from former clients accusing her of malpractice. It was all too much.

Her heart raced as she opened her laptop. She hadn't checked the news in days, but she knew what she would find. More headlines, more accusations. But as she typed her name into the search bar, one particular article stood out:

"Former Client Speaks: Catherine Faber Ruined My Life."

She clicked on it, her eyes scanning the words, each one hitting her like a punch to the gut. The woman in the article—Jessica—had been one of her first high-profile cases. She had come to Catherine after a messy divorce, claiming emotional abuse. Catherine had taken her under her wing, convinced her that she had been a victim, that her husband had manipulated her. But now, Jessica was saying that none of it was true. That Catherine had planted the idea in her head, that she had left therapy more broken than when she had entered it.

Catherine closed the laptop and buried her face in her hands. The shame was overwhelming, suffocating. How many more would come forward? How many more lives had she ruined, all because she couldn't let go of her own trauma?

The wine wasn't enough anymore. The numbness it brought wasn't enough to drown out the guilt, the crushing realization that she had become the very thing she had fought against. She reached for the pill bottle on the counter, the one she had been prescribed after the panic attacks started. She hadn't touched it in weeks, but now, it seemed like the only option.

She took one, then another, chasing them down with the last of the wine. The dizziness came quickly, and she welcomed it. Maybe now, she could finally stop thinking, finally stop feeling.

As she lay down on the couch, the room spinning around her, Catherine Faber closed her eyes and let the darkness take over.

Chapter 11: Facing the Truth

The air in the café was thick with tension as Catherine Faber sat across from Vanessa Hale for what she knew would be their final meeting. The usual café sounds—coffee machines hissing, cutlery clinking, light chatter—felt muted, as if the world around them was holding its breath. Catherine's fingers traced the rim of her coffee cup, her mind spinning with the weight of the accusations and the collapse of her carefully curated life.

Vanessa looked different. Gone was the vulnerable socialite she had once taken under her wing. Now, Vanessa sat across from her with cold detachment, dressed in the latest high-end fashion, exuding a confidence that Catherine found unsettling. It was a transformation Catherine had helped foster, but this version of Vanessa was not what she had envisioned.

"I suppose you know why I asked you to meet me," Vanessa said, her voice measured, lacking the tremor that had characterized their previous conversations. Catherine glanced up, locking eyes with Vanessa, trying to see a hint of the woman she had once fiercely defended.

"I have an idea," Catherine replied, her voice quiet but tense.

"You've been lying to yourself, Catherine," Vanessa said bluntly. "Just like you've been lying to everyone else. And now it's all falling apart."

Catherine flinched at the accusation, a familiar chill running down her spine. It was the same feeling she had experienced when she was a child, sitting across from her father during one of his vicious tirades. Her stomach twisted as she felt the walls closing in. For weeks, she had been trying to distance herself from Vanessa, from the case, from the mounting accusations. But now, she had no choice but to face the truth head-on.

"You were the one who lied," Catherine snapped, her voice sharper than she intended. "You're the one who exaggerated everything, who wanted to paint Evan as some monster for your own gain. I tried to help you. I gave you a platform to be heard."

Vanessa leaned back in her chair, a small, bitter smile forming on her lips. "You gave me exactly what I needed, Catherine. A story. A perfect victim narrative. And you needed it too, didn't you? You needed me to be the victim so you could play the savior."

The words cut through Catherine like a blade. She had spent years building her career on the idea that she was helping women like Vanessa. She had dedicated her life to saving women from their abusers, offering them a way out, a voice when they felt silenced. But now, everything was unraveling, and Catherine was struggling to differentiate between her noble intentions and the damage she had caused.

"You were a victim," Catherine said, her voice trembling as she tried to regain control of the conversation. "Evan—"

"Evan never hit me," Vanessa interrupted, her voice growing colder. "He never raised a hand to me. But you convinced me that he did. You took my doubts, my frustrations with my marriage, and turned them into something they weren't. You made me believe I was trapped. And once I started going along with it, I couldn't stop. The media, the attention, it all became so... intoxicating."

Catherine sat frozen, her heart pounding in her chest. She opened her mouth to protest, but the words wouldn't come. Was Vanessa telling the truth? Or was this just another manipulation in a long line of lies? Doubt crept into her mind, twisting her thoughts like a vise.

Vanessa leaned forward, her eyes dark and unyielding. "Do you even remember how it started, Catherine? You pushed me. You wanted me to embellish, to make it bigger than it was. You didn't just guide me—you shaped my story, twisted it until even I couldn't tell what was real anymore."

Catherine's hands began to shake. She had always believed that her methods were necessary, that the ends justified the means. Her clients needed her, and sometimes, that meant helping them see the truth, even if it took a little coaxing. But as Vanessa's words echoed in her mind, Catherine felt the fragile foundation of her career crumbling beneath her.

"I didn't twist anything," Catherine whispered, her voice barely audible. "I helped you. I gave you the strength to leave him."

Vanessa's laugh was sharp, filled with contempt. "You gave me the strength to lie, Catherine. And now, look where we are. My story is falling apart, and I have no intention of going down alone. You're coming with me."

The café seemed to close in on Catherine as Vanessa's words sank in. She had been so sure, so convinced that she was doing the right thing. But now, confronted with the truth, she couldn't escape the gnawing doubt that had been eating away at her for months. Had she pushed too hard? Had she manipulated Vanessa, just like her father had manipulated her mother?

Vanessa leaned back in her chair, crossing her arms. "This is your fault as much as it's mine. Maybe more. You projected your own issues onto me, onto all your clients. You're the one who's broken, Catherine. And now, the world's going to see it."

Catherine's mind raced as she tried to find a way out, a way to salvage what was left of her reputation. But deep down, she knew Vanessa was right. She had crossed a line, blurred the boundaries between therapist and victim, between truth and manipulation. And now, there was no going back.

"You're not innocent in this," Catherine said, her voice barely a whisper. "You played your part."

Vanessa smirked, her eyes gleaming with satisfaction. "Oh, I know. But you're the one they're going to blame. You're the expert. You're the one who was supposed to know better."

The weight of Vanessa's words crushed Catherine, leaving her gasping for air. She had spent her life running from her past, from the scars her father had left on her psyche. But now, as her world fell apart, Catherine realized she had become the very thing she despised—a manipulator, a user, just like her father.

"I'll make sure the truth comes out," Vanessa said, standing up and grabbing her purse. "I'll tell everyone what you did.

And trust me, they'll believe me. After all, you're the one with a history of pushing people into believing things that aren't real."

Catherine sat there, frozen, as Vanessa walked out of the café, leaving her alone with the crushing weight of her guilt. The world outside continued to move, oblivious to the implosion happening in Catherine's life.

For the first time in her career, Catherine couldn't hide behind her professional mask. The cracks in her façade were too deep, too wide to ignore. She had spent so long building up the image of the perfect savior, but now, all that was left was a woman who had lost sight of the truth—about her clients, her career, and herself.

As the minutes ticked by, Catherine finally stood up, her legs shaky as she made her way to the door. The truth had been staring her in the face all along, but she had been too blinded by her own trauma to see it. Now, she had no choice but to face the consequences of her actions.

The final confrontation with Vanessa had left Catherine with a devastating realization: she had spent her life fighting against the wrong enemy. The real monster wasn't the abusers she had vowed to protect her clients from—it was the unresolved pain and anger that had been festering inside her for decades.

And now, it was too late to turn back.

Catherine sat in her office, staring blankly at the wall, the muffled hum of the city outside barely registering in her consciousness. The space, once a refuge for her—filled with awards, degrees, and accolades—now felt oppressive, almost mocking in its silence. Her hands trembled slightly as she adjusted the frame of a photo on her desk: her and Vanessa

Hale, smiling after the trial, a moment frozen in time when Catherine had been on top of the world. Now, it was all crumbling, and Catherine could feel the weight of the truth she had been running from her entire life pressing down on her.

Her eyes darted to the clock on the wall. The meeting with Vanessa had ended less than an hour ago, but the echoes of Vanessa's words still reverberated in her mind, each one a barb that dug deeper into her psyche.

"You pushed me to lie, Catherine. You wanted me to be your perfect victim, and I let you. You're no different from the men you claim to fight against."

Vanessa's voice had been steady, cold. There had been no hesitation in her accusation, no remorse. And now, sitting alone, Catherine couldn't shake the feeling that Vanessa was right.

The truth had always been there, simmering beneath the surface, but Catherine had become a master at burying it. She had built an entire career around her ability to help women escape abusive relationships, but in reality, she had been escaping her own trauma the entire time. Her father's face flickered in her mind, his cruel words, his manipulation, the way he had twisted her mother's life into something unrecognizable. And then, her mother's suicide—a moment that had shattered Catherine's world and set her on the path she had been walking ever since. A path that, she now realized, had led her right back to the same manipulation and control she had vowed to fight.

She had always told herself that her work was about justice, about helping women find their strength, but the truth was far more complicated. Catherine's need to save her clients had never been about them. It had always been about her. It had been about rewriting the story of her mother's life, about creating a world where the weak were no longer victims. But in doing so, she had crossed a line—a line she had been blind to for years.

The door to her office creaked open, and her assistant, Julia, hesitantly stepped in. "Dr. Faber, you have a call from—"

"Not now, Julia," Catherine cut her off, her voice sharper than she intended. Julia flinched slightly, then nodded and slipped out of the room, leaving Catherine alone with her thoughts once again.

Catherine's gaze fell to the stack of files on her desk. Client after client—women who had come to her seeking guidance, seeking validation. She had given it to them, but at what cost? How many of their stories had she twisted to fit her own narrative? How many of them had she led down a path they might not have chosen on their own?

Her mind drifted back to a session from years ago, with a woman named Lauren. Lauren had come to Catherine confused, unsure if her husband's behavior was abusive or just the result of a strained marriage. Catherine had been quick to label it abuse. She had seen the signs, the subtle cues, the same ones she had lived through with her father. But now, in hindsight, she wasn't so sure. Had Lauren really been a victim? Or had Catherine pushed her into seeing herself as one because it was easier to believe that than to confront the nuances of her marriage?

The realization was like a punch to the gut. Catherine had built her entire identity around being the savior, the one who could see the truth even when her clients couldn't. But the truth wasn't always black and white. In her quest to save others, she had projected her own trauma onto them, forcing them into roles they hadn't asked for.

Her thoughts were interrupted by the shrill ring of her phone. For a moment, she considered ignoring it, but something compelled her to pick up the receiver.

"Catherine Faber," she said, her voice hollow.

"Dr. Faber, it's Rebecca Adams," a familiar voice said on the other end. Rebecca had been one of Catherine's earliest clients, a woman who had come to her in the midst of a bitter divorce, convinced that her husband had been emotionally abusive. Catherine had helped her win the case, had been there every step of the way as Rebecca rebuilt her life. But now, Rebecca's tone was different, hesitant.

"I... I've been thinking a lot about our sessions," Rebecca said, her voice wavering. "About the things we talked about, the way you helped me see things."

Catherine's heart sank. She knew what was coming.

"I don't know if I can trust my memories anymore," Rebecca continued. "It's like... it's like you put these ideas in my head, and I believed them because I wanted to. But now, I'm not so sure. Was it really abuse, or was I just going through a rough time? Did I ruin my marriage because I listened to you?"

Catherine closed her eyes, a wave of nausea rolling through her. She had no answer for Rebecca. How could she? The truth was, she didn't know anymore.

"I'm sorry," Rebecca whispered. "I just needed to say that."

The line went dead, leaving Catherine with nothing but the silence and the crushing weight of her guilt.

She stood up from her desk, pacing the room, her mind racing. She had spent years convincing herself that she was doing the right thing, that she was helping these women. But now, all she could see were the lies, the manipulations, the blurred lines between truth and fiction. She had crossed ethical boundaries without even realizing it, and now the consequences were catching up to her.

Vanessa's words echoed in her mind again: "You're no different from the men you claim to fight against."

Catherine's breath caught in her throat as the full weight of that statement hit her. She had become the very thing she despised. She had wielded her power over her clients, shaping their narratives to fit her own agenda, just as her father had done to her mother. And in doing so, she had betrayed the very people she had sworn to protect.

The walls of her office seemed to close in around her, the air growing thick and suffocating. She couldn't stay here. Not in this place that had once been a symbol of her success but was now a constant reminder of her failures.

Without thinking, she grabbed her coat and keys and headed for the door. She needed air. She needed space to think, to process, to figure out what came next.

As she stepped out onto the street, the cool evening breeze hit her face, but it did little to clear the fog in her mind. She walked aimlessly, her feet carrying her through the city streets, past the bustling crowds and the glowing storefronts. The world around her was moving, but Catherine felt frozen, trapped in her own guilt and self-loathing.

She found herself at the park, the same park she used to visit with her mother before everything had fallen apart. The memories flooded back—her mother's soft laughter, the way she had always made Catherine feel safe, even when things at home were anything but. And then the day it had all ended, the day her mother had taken her own life, leaving Catherine alone with her father's cruelty.

Catherine sank onto a bench, her head in her hands. She had spent her entire life trying to fix what had been broken that day, trying to save other women in the way she hadn't been able to save her mother. But in the process, she had lost herself. She had become a victim of her own trauma, and in her desperation to make things right, she had turned others into victims as well.

A sob escaped her throat, and for the first time in years, Catherine allowed herself to cry. Not just for her mother, but for herself, for the woman she had become. The realization was devastating, but it was also freeing in a way. For the first time, she saw herself clearly—not as a hero, not as a savior, but as a flawed, broken person who had made terrible mistakes.

The tears flowed freely as Catherine sat alone in the darkness, her body shaking with the force of her grief. She had spent so long trying to be perfect, trying to control everything around her, but now, there was nothing left to control. The truth had finally caught up to her, and there was no escaping it.

As the night stretched on, Catherine's sobs gradually subsided, leaving her drained but strangely calm. She didn't know what came next, didn't know how she would begin to atone for the damage she had caused. But one thing was certain: she could no longer run from the truth.

Chapter 12: The Fall

Catherine Faber stared at the headlines that flickered across her computer screen, the sharp glow of the screen highlighting the weariness etched into her face. "Disgraced Psychologist Sued for Manipulation," screamed one title. "Hero to Villain: How Catherine Faber Destroyed Lives," said another. She had once commanded the admiration of the public, her reputation as an advocate for women a beacon of hope, but now she was reduced to this: a pariah.

The lawsuits were piling up, a relentless wave of legal notices that threatened to swallow her whole. Former clients were coming forward with claims of coercion, manipulation, and emotional abuse. It was a nightmare that Catherine couldn't wake up from, the kind that eroded everything she had built—every accolade, every word of praise, every ounce of respect. Gone.

Sitting in her dimly lit apartment, Catherine's mind wandered back to the beginning, to the woman who had set the wheels of her downfall in motion: Vanessa Hale. The socialite had played her part well, selling the story of a battered wife desperate to escape her powerful husband, a tale that Catherine had latched onto with fervor. It was a story Catherine had wanted to believe, perhaps needed to believe.

Vanessa was a victim, she had told herself. But now, after everything, Catherine couldn't tell if Vanessa had ever been a victim at all—or if the real victim had always been Catherine herself.

The emails from her lawyer had gone unanswered for days. Catherine couldn't bear to read them. She knew what they said—recommendations to settle, to avoid court. But every time she thought about giving in, the bile rose in her throat. Settle meant admitting guilt, and Catherine wasn't sure she was ready to do that. Not yet. Deep down, she clung to the belief that she had helped people, that the women she'd worked with had needed her guidance. But as the days passed, that belief grew thinner, more fragile, until it felt like a lie she was telling herself to survive.

Her phone buzzed again, dragging her back to the present. It was another message from her lawyer: "Catherine, we need to talk. The firm is recommending we settle. You won't survive this if we go to trial. Call me back." She let the phone fall from her hand and stared blankly out the window. The apartment, once a sanctuary filled with reminders of her success, now felt suffocating, the walls closing in. The shelves that had held plaques and framed newspaper clippings of her achievements were empty, stripped of the accolades that had once defined her. The emptiness was a fitting metaphor for her life now.

Catherine rose from the couch, her legs unsteady, and walked to the kitchen. The ticking of the clock on the wall seemed louder in the silence, each second an accusation. She reached for the bottle of wine she had opened the night before, the last of many she had gone through in recent weeks. The taste was bitter on her tongue, much like everything else in her life now.

As she poured herself another glass, her mind drifted to the lawsuit that had broken everything wide open—Rachel Collins, the first client to come forward publicly. Rachel had been one of Catherine's success stories, or so Catherine had thought. She had come to Catherine bruised and broken, a woman who had suffered at the hands of a manipulative and controlling partner. Catherine had been proud of her work with Rachel, of the way she had helped her regain her confidence and take control of her life.

But that confidence, it seemed, had come at a price. Rachel claimed now that Catherine had pushed her too far, convincing her that her partner was more abusive than he truly was. It was a story that echoed in the testimonies of other former clients, each one more damning than the last.

The wine sloshed in her glass as Catherine walked back to the living room, her movements unsteady. She sank into the couch, the weight of her guilt pressing down on her chest. Guilt she hadn't allowed herself to fully acknowledge before. She had always been the savior, the one who helped others escape their demons. But what if, in doing so, she had become the demon herself?

Her phone buzzed again, but this time it wasn't her lawyer. It was a message from a number she didn't recognize: "You're going to pay for what you did." Catherine's pulse quickened as she stared at the words on the screen. This wasn't the first message of its kind, and she knew it wouldn't be the last. The online harassment had started as soon as the media had turned on her, angry voices calling for her to be held accountable, to be punished for the lives she had allegedly destroyed.

There had been a time when Catherine had felt invincible, when the support of her clients and the public had made her feel like she could do no wrong. But that time was over. Now, the world saw her as a villain, and Catherine wasn't sure they were entirely wrong.

She took a long sip of wine, letting the warmth spread through her, dulling the edge of the fear that had been gnawing at her for weeks. But the relief was temporary. It always was.

The knock on the door startled her, the sound sharp and insistent. Catherine froze, her mind racing. She wasn't expecting anyone. The knocking came again, louder this time, and she felt her heart begin to race. Her first thought was that it was the media, desperate for another headline to feed the public's insatiable appetite for scandal. But when she approached the door and peered through the peephole, she saw no cameras, no reporters.

It was Vanessa Hale.

Catherine's breath caught in her throat. What was Vanessa doing here? The last time they had spoken, Vanessa had publicly turned against her, accusing Catherine of manipulating her into fabricating her story. Catherine had been left to bear the brunt of the public's anger while Vanessa had walked away, playing the victim once again.

Slowly, Catherine opened the door, her mind spinning with questions. Vanessa stood on the other side, looking as composed and polished as ever. But there was something in her eyes—something Catherine couldn't quite place.

"Catherine," Vanessa said, her voice smooth but cold. "We need to talk."

For a moment, Catherine considered slamming the door in her face. But the curiosity was too strong. She stepped aside, letting Vanessa in, and closed the door behind her.

Vanessa didn't waste any time. "I know what you're thinking," she said, her tone flat. "You think I ruined your life. That I used you to get what I wanted."

Catherine didn't respond. She wasn't sure what to say. Of course, she blamed Vanessa. Vanessa had lied, manipulated the truth to serve her own ends, and left Catherine to take the fall. But deep down, Catherine knew it wasn't that simple. She had played a part in her own downfall, and now she was paying the price.

Vanessa took a seat on the couch, crossing her legs. "I didn't come here to apologize," she said, her eyes locking onto Catherine's. "I came here because I think we both know that this isn't over. Not for you. Not for me."

Catherine swallowed, her throat dry. "What do you want, Vanessa?"

Vanessa smiled, but it didn't reach her eyes. "I want to make sure you understand something. You and I, we're not so different. You may have convinced yourself that you were helping people, that you were some kind of hero. But in the end, you were just using them. Just like I used you."

The words hit Catherine like a punch to the gut. She had always prided herself on being different, on fighting for the vulnerable. But now, in the face of her own ruin, she couldn't deny the truth in Vanessa's words.

"We both wanted power," Vanessa continued. "Control. You over your clients, me over my life. The difference is, I never pretended to be anything other than what I am. You, on the other hand, hid behind a facade of morality. But look where that got you."

Catherine felt her hands tremble, the glass of wine slipping from her fingers and shattering on the floor. The sound echoed in the silence, but neither woman flinched.

Vanessa stood, smoothing her dress. "I'll be leaving town soon," she said, her tone casual. "But I wanted to leave you with one last piece of advice. Stop pretending you're the victim. You're not. You never were."

With that, Vanessa walked to the door, pausing only to glance back at Catherine one last time. "Good luck, Catherine. You're going to need it."

And then she was gone, leaving Catherine alone in the wreckage of her life.

The clock continued to tick in the silence, each second a reminder of the choices Catherine had made, the lives she had shattered—including her own. She stood there, staring at the broken glass on the floor, the weight of her guilt finally crashing down on her. There was no escaping it now. The truth was out, and Catherine had no one left to blame but herself.

Catherine sat in the dimly lit room, the walls closing in on her. The sound of the rain tapping against the window was relentless, but she found no comfort in its rhythm. She was alone—truly alone for the first time in years. No clients, no admirers, no reporters seeking her expert opinion. All she had left was the overwhelming silence of her downfall. Her hands shook as she reached for the glass of water on the table, her reflection distorted in its surface. She hardly recognized the woman staring back at her.

Her phone buzzed. Another notification—probably another article, another analysis of her disgrace. The media had latched onto her like a predator on wounded prey. They weren't satisfied with just watching her fall—they wanted to dismantle every last piece of her reputation, her legacy, her life.

She had fought so hard, hadn't she? She'd fought for Vanessa, for all her clients, and even for herself. Or had she been fighting against something else entirely—her own demons, her own past? The truth gnawed at her now, undeniable, unrelenting. Vanessa's words echoed in her mind, a poisonous refrain she couldn't shake: You're just as bad as them. You're just as bad as the men you claim to protect us from.

She stood and paced the room, the air heavy with the smell of stale coffee and sleepless nights. How had it come to this? How had she let herself become so blind? She had always believed in her work, in her methods. She had always told herself she was doing good, saving lives. But that was the lie, wasn't it? The lie she'd told herself to keep from facing the truth—that she had been manipulating her clients as much as anyone had ever manipulated her.

Her father's voice came back to her, as clear as if he were standing in the room. "You'll never be good enough, Catherine. You'll always be a failure, just like your mother."

Catherine closed her eyes, trying to block out the sound, but it was useless. The memories flooded back—the nights when her father would sit in his chair, staring at her with those cold, unfeeling eyes, tearing her down piece by piece. And her mother, her poor, broken mother, who had tried so hard to protect her, only to end up taking her own life.

That had been the turning point, hadn't it? The moment when Catherine had decided she would never be like her father. She would help people, lift them up, make sure no one ever felt as helpless as she had. But in trying to fight against him, she had become a reflection of him. She had become the abuser she had sworn to despise.

Vanessa had been right. They had both used each other, but Catherine had been the one pulling the strings. Vanessa might have wanted the fame, the attention, but Catherine had wanted something deeper—validation. She needed to prove to the world, to herself, that she could save people, that she could fix what had been broken inside her. And in doing so, she had destroyed lives.

Her clients' faces flashed before her eyes. Women who had come to her for help, for guidance, for clarity. And what had she given them? False memories, twisted perceptions of their own experiences. She had convinced them they were victims because it was the only way she knew how to see the world. If they weren't victims, then what was she?

Her phone buzzed again, but this time she ignored it. It didn't matter anymore. Nothing did.

She walked to the window and stared out at the rain-soaked street below. Life was still moving out there. Cars rushed by, people huddled under umbrellas, unaware of the storm raging inside her. Her entire life's work was crumbling around her, and yet the world continued on as if nothing had changed.

She thought of her mother again—how she had once stood at a window much like this one, staring out at a world that seemed indifferent to her suffering. Catherine had vowed that day that she would never let herself be consumed by the same despair. But here she was, standing on the edge of the same abyss.

The lawsuits were piling up. Former clients, emboldened by Vanessa's revelations, had come forward with their own stories of manipulation, coercion, and false memories. They weren't wrong. Catherine knew that now. She had crossed lines, ethical and moral, in her pursuit of control. She had projected her own trauma onto others, using them as pawns in her battle with the ghosts of her past.

Her professional license had been revoked. The malpractice suits were inevitable, and the legal battles that lay ahead would be long and brutal. Her savings were dwindling, and soon she would have nothing left—not even the ability to defend herself. She had been stripped of everything: her career, her reputation, her purpose.

The final blow had come just days ago, when Vanessa had gone public with her confession. She had sat in a glossy TV studio, dressed in black, her voice trembling as she told the world how Catherine had coerced her into embellishing her story. How Catherine had made her believe that her marriage had been abusive when, in truth, it had merely been unfulfilling. Vanessa had painted herself as a victim once again, but this time, the villain wasn't Evan Hale—it was Catherine.

The public had eaten it up. Headlines screamed about Catherine's downfall, her manipulation, her lies. The woman who had built her career on helping others had been exposed as a fraud. And now, there was nothing left but the wreckage.

Catherine sat back down, the weight of it all pressing down on her chest. She thought of the women she had hurt, the lives she had shattered. She had believed she was helping them, but in reality, she had been using them to fill the void inside her. She had wanted to fix them because she couldn't fix herself.

She reached for a pen and a piece of paper. There was one thing left to do—one last act of control, one final decision she could make for herself. She couldn't undo the damage she had done, but she could make sure that no one else was hurt by her actions. She could finally take responsibility for the monster she had become.

The words came slowly at first, then faster, as if they had been waiting all along to be released.

To those I've hurt, she wrote. I'm sorry. I thought I was helping, but I was wrong. I let my own pain, my own trauma, blind me to the truth. I pushed you to see yourselves as victims because that's how I saw myself. I wanted to save you, but I only ended up hurting you. I became the very thing I despised, and for that, I will never forgive myself.

She paused, her hand trembling. The rain outside had slowed to a drizzle, and the world seemed eerily still. For the first time in a long time, Catherine felt a strange sense of peace. It wasn't the peace of absolution—she knew she didn't deserve that—but it was the peace of knowing that her story was finally over.

She signed the letter and folded it neatly, placing it on the table. Then she stood and walked to the window, opening it wide. The cool air rushed in, filling the room with the scent of rain.

Catherine took one last look at the city below, at the life she had once known. And then, without a second thought, she stepped out into the night.

The rain swallowed her whole.

Don't miss out!

Visit the website below and you can sign up to receive emails whenever Michael Ferguson publishes a new book. There's no charge and no obligation.

https://books2read.com/r/B-A-CKNW-DQJZE

BOOKS 2 READ

Connecting independent readers to independent writers.

Did you love *Perfect Victim*? Then you should read *Shattered Crown*[1] by Michael Ferguson!

[2]

In the war-torn empire of Rethnor, the gods have been silent for centuries, and their once-mighty temples lie in ruins. Rival kingdoms vie for control, while an ancient, unspeakable evil stirs beneath the surface, threatening to plunge the world into eternal darkness.

Kade, a disgraced warrior-priest known as the Holy Blade, lives in exile after betraying the very gods he once served. Haunted by guilt and visions of the gods' fall, he is offered a chance at redemption: recover the legendary Crown of the

---

1. https://books2read.com/u/4AMQ0q

2. https://books2read.com/u/4AMQ0q

Fallen, a powerful relic said to have the ability to resurrect the gods and restore balance to the world.

But Kade knows a terrible secret—he was complicit in the gods' downfall, and their destruction was not what it seemed. As he embarks on his dangerous quest, a ragtag group of outcasts and misfits joins him: Mira, a powerful mage with a hidden past; Tyra, a young thief who claims to have seen the gods in her dreams; and Sorin, a mercenary with questionable loyalties. Together, they navigate treacherous lands, from desolate wastelands to haunted forests, seeking the Crown's true location.

As the group draws closer to their goal, Kade's darkest secret begins to unravel. His bloodline is bound to the ancient evil—the very force the gods sacrificed themselves to contain. The Crown, far from being a tool for salvation, is revealed to be the key to unleashing this malevolent entity upon the world. And the only way to stop it is for Kade to make the ultimate sacrifice: his own daughter, Lyra, who was thought lost long ago, but is now revealed to be the vessel for the ancient evil.

Caught between love and duty, redemption and damnation, Kade must decide whether to save the world by destroying everything he holds dear or release the evil that could end all life. As alliances fracture and dark forces close in, Kade and his companions face an impossible choice: will they fight for a future built on sacrifice, or will they surrender to the forces of darkness?

In Shattered Crown, the fate of the world lies in the hands of a man whose very bloodline is cursed, a group of misfits bound by fragile trust, and a relic that could either save or doom them all. This epic fantasy blends intense action, moral complexity, and world-shattering stakes into a tale that will leave readers breathless. As Kade's journey unfolds, nothing is as it seems, and the ultimate question remains—can redemption truly be found, or are some sins unforgivable?

www.ingramcontent.com/pod-product-compliance
Lightning Source LLC
Chambersburg PA
CBHW071318130726
47996CB00002B/526